Happy Reading

Jean Selch

JESSIE-BY-THE-SEA

A Story of Westport

ISBN: 978-0-578-61660-5
Printed in the United States of America by
Grand Mesa Graphics, Inc
Grand Junction, CO 81501

JESSIE-BY-THE-SEA

1

Midnight, the A-1 café was busy. The café used up about a fourth of a building on the main street of Westport looking out over the docks and harbor. It was a white stucco with red trim building. The front door was locked, but looking through the large front steamed up windows, the comings and goings of two workers could occasionally be seen. The ell shaped seating area had tables with flatware rolled into napkins at every chair. Sugar, salt and pepper shakers were full and waiting for the crowd.

Few people were downtown Westport at this hour. One who was, was standing at the door looking through the glass. He knocked and waited. The man inside looked around the corner. The knocker pantomimed a cup of coffee.

"O.K., Jim. Hang on."

The speaker came to the door with a coffee pot and, sure enough, the man had his own cup ready for the fill. It was a normal part of their routine. Not really a problem in a small town.

"Thanks, Harry. You're saving my life."

Harry nodded and smiled and returned to the kitchen area. He was a tall and thin man with a perpetually pleasant expression on his face. The blue eyes and thinning hair, together with his apron gave a very normal picture for a cook. He owned the A-1 and worked very long hours.

The two kitchen workers were very busy. By four o'clock, the restaurant would be crammed with hungry fishermen wanting some breakfast and a lot of hot coffee. Breakfast would not take a lot of prep cooking, but lunch and supper would and Jessie was busy with a case of lettuce.

"How much lettuce do you need?" she called out to Harry.

It was two o'clock in the morning and Jessie was busy at her prep cooking job. She was dressed in clean blue jeans and a short sleeved white blouse. Her abundant chestnut hair was covered by a hair net, her eyes were blue and very alert. She wore a normal expression for her – one side of her mouth was up in a half smile and she was humming Turn Turn Turn to herself. The half smile usually meant something was perplexing her. She had a smudge of flour on one cheek from making biscuits.

Harry looked over at her. She was a good worker and was very clean and reliable. He laughed to himself though because he knew she would have a fit when she discovered the flour on her face. Clean and neat was her style. However, she was very small, even though she had turned fifteen that spring. She was five foot nothing and maybe weighed eighty-five pounds. Altogether, she was a very good employee. She also was very quiet and seldom said more than yup or nope. Asking about the lettuce was a long sentence for her. He laughed to himself again. She was definitely different from most fifteen-year old girls.

"We'll need a lot. I am expecting a big crowd today. We'll be serving a lot of salads and such. So, shred at least half of that case. That should be enough," he said to himself as well as to Jessie.

Jessie nodded her head in response and kept on shredding the lettuce heads. She was very alert.

During the winter, many of the Alaskan fishermen brought their boats to Westport for storage until their next season. The harbor itself was deep and could handle the very large oceangoing boats. These huge boats were loaded and unloaded on the opposite side of the harbor from Westport.

Altogether, because Jessie spent her summers in Westport, she was used to the crowding and confusion.

At a quarter of five, she finished and took her apron to the clothes hamper. "See you next Thursday," she called out to Harry. He waved and she stepped out the back door to discover her stepmom waiting for her in the parking area.

The sun was up and the day looked to be cloudless and mild. A pretty typical day for Westport in the summertime.

She crossed over to the car and opened the passenger door. The car was running and the heater was on. Her step-mother, Betty, was still dressed in a sweater with a coat and hat. She wore a bright lipstick but no other makeup. "Hi, Jessica. Have a good night working?" she asked. Jessie was surprised to see her there. Her dad usually picked her up. Betty was kept pretty busy with the baby, so she rarely picked her up from work.

"Yup," Jessie responded. "Where's Dad?" she added with a smile.

Betty smiled back and said, "He's trying to find a deck-hand for the day. Dennis is unavailable ... again. Your dad is on the phone at this odd hour trying to locate Kenny or someone. So, I volunteered to come pick you up."

"Dad is sure having problems with his deckhands this summer," Jessie commented. Betty nodded in agreement.

Jessie's half smile appeared as she thought to herself. "It's too bad I can't do the deckhanding. It sure pays better than restaurant work."

"These teenage boys are not very reliable, sometimes." Betty continued. "Bob says they have an attitude of the world owing them a living."

"Some of them do a pretty good job. I've heard Dad talk about them," Jessie commented.

The trip home took about twenty minutes. The house was set on the edge of the harbor with great views of the water. There was a small apartment over the garage, which is where Jessie stayed when she was with her father. School time was spent in Seattle with her mother and stepfather and another younger brother. "A modern family," her mother would say.

When they arrived home, Bob Martin was dressed and ready to leave for the day.

"Did you find someone to deckhand?" Betty asked.

"Yes," he replied. "George can come, but just for two days." He was gathering up his lunch and a couple of thermoses of coffee.

"The baby didn't make a peep but I'll bet he'll wake up wet and hungry soon enough. Well, maybe not wet. He's getting better about that." He looked at his wife and gave her a quick kiss on the cheek and started putting on his jacket. "Thanks for picking up Jess for me."

"You have a good night at the old A1?" he asked Jessie.

She nodded. Her dad was dark haired and blue eyed, wore glasses and usually had a pipe in his mouth. He was square jawed and a good looking man. When he was on the boat with his hat, pipe and glasses, he looked the part of a sea captain. He acted pretty calm, but she knew he was feeling hassled.

She looked down at her feet and struggled with herself. "I need some courage," she thought to herself. She had had an idea for some time now and was aware her dad might not take kindly to her suggestion. Then again, he might think it was ok. Jessie really had no idea how he would react. So, she steeled herself and blurted out, "Dad. I am fifteen now and am old enough to deckhand. I would like the job."

There was total silence. Of the three hundred and fifty salmon charter boats with about eight hundred employees leaving the Westport docks each day, maybe there were ten to twelve women working and several of them were wives. It was a man's job. Period.

Bob looked at Jessie. He put both hands to his face and rubbed it as if he was very tired. Jessie was so very small and deckhanding was tough work and made for long working days with little time for breaks. He did not want to say no to her, but her becoming a deckhand was not very probable. She was just too small. He debated with himself.

"I'll tell you what. Let's talk about this this evening. I need time to think about it. Truthfully, I think you're too small to do the work. But we'll talk about it tonight."

He shook his head and scrunched his shoulders.

Jessie nodded.

"Also," he paused for effect, "I don't think it is good form for deckhands to have a dab of flour on their cheek." He left for the docks still chuckling to himself.

2

Betty looked at her. "Well, he didn't say no. That's a good sign."

"Yup."

Jessie felt her face and found the flour on her cheek. She laughed and went to wash her face. She had a piece of cheese for breakfast, bathed and went straight to bed. Jessie slept fitfully for the rest of the morning and was groggy and tired that afternoon.

She dug through her supply of jeans and blouses. Then looked at the sweaters she had in her drawers. It looked like there was adequate clothes to wear if she did get the job.

It seemed like forever before she and Betty heard the car coming down the driveway that evening. Bob came in the door and gave Betty a quick kiss and then took off his jacket.

"Hey, Sam," he said to the baby who was busy with a toy baseball bat.

"Hi, Jess."

He put the thermos bottles in the kitchen and came back to the living room with a beer in his hand. He cleaned out his pipe, loaded it and lit it. After his first puff, he sighed and smiled at the group.

"You still want to deckhand, Jessie?"

She nodded. It was not just a slight movement of her head, but two firm nods.

"Well, I've given this a lot of thought today. We can try you out for a couple of days starting Friday. Truthfully, you are too small. Even if you were a boy, I would not want to hire you. But it is possible you can manage."

"We'll talk about your being hired permanently after the two days. It will be my decision as to your continuing with NO argument from you. One day may be as much as you will ever want to do, anyway." He paused. "That O.K. with you?" he added smiling.

Jessie began hopping up and down. Her braids bounced. Friday was the day after tomorrow and she knew, just knew, that she could handle the work. The money was very good for summer work.

Bob laughed. Jessica was the picture of excitement. He knew that getting her oriented to deckhanding responsibilities was going to make for a long couple of days and that the work would probably be too demanding for her to do, but showing her what he did for a living would be good.

"There's a pair of Kelly Jansens on the boat that we can take down a bit for you to wear. You may look a bit like a clown for your first day, what with the legs being rolled up and the top straps shortened. But I suspect you will survive until we find out if you want to do this job for the rest of the summer."

"This O.K. with you?"

Jessie nodded and headed back to her room. Betty followed her back. "What are Kelly Jansens?" Betty asked.

"Waterproof bib overalls. They make all kinds of waterproof coats, hats and stuff," Jessie responded.

"I'll make a trip to Aberdeen if Dad lets me have the job. I'll get work boots. The rest I can get in Westport. Dark green is a good color and I'll get the sou'wester and the rest to match."

"That bright Coast Guard orange color is too much. Don't like it at all," she mused to herself. Then she laughed. "I'll have to go to Penney's boys department to find leather shoes my size. That's the kind I'll need," she told Betty.

Betty smiled, "Shopping is hard work," she quipped.

It was early July and being on the ocean was cold. She planned on wearing two sweaters. If it was rainy, she could wear her rain gear and if it was warm she could always shed her rain gear and top sweater. "I need heavier shoes. But for now, my tennies will do. I can wash them as I go along. This should work out," she thought to herself. And then she remembered, "I need to remember to stop by the A-1 and ask Harry to find someone else to do my job."

Her little brother, Sam, was about a year old and getting into lots of trouble with his newfound ability to walk and talk. He was pretty much following Jessie around as she got her clothes organized.

Jessie stopped and looked at the toddler. "Sam, you are sure easy to trip over." Sam smiled as if this was the nicest compliment he could receive.

Jessie reached down and picked him up. He was chunky and wiggly and she adored him. "Gessie hurry?" he asked. He had trouble with the J sound, so she became Gessie. "Yup," she responded and nuzzled him. "Gessie is going to go to work for Dad."

Sam looked at her quizzically. He didn't understand what she was saying but he knew Jessie was happy.

"Work for Dad," he echoed back to her.

When Bob returned that following evening, he had the rain-gear with him. They rolled up the pant-legs and shortened the straps as much as possible. They still flopped on Jessie. Bob scratched his head. Loose clothing was not a good idea on a fishing boat.

"Do you have a belt somewhere?" he asked Jessie.

Jessie shook her head no and wondered about just using some kind of rope. "I'm definitely going to look like a clown," she thought to herself.

Then Betty piped up, "You know. I might have just the thing." She left for a moment and returned with a coat belt. It was perfect.

"Thanks, Betty," Jessie said. "You just saved me tons of trouble."

That night just before she was ready to go to bed, she made herself three cheese sandwiches and they, plus three Three Musketeer candy bars, would be her breakfast and lunch on the **Jazzer**.

3

About 5:00 the next morning, Jessie and Captain Martin headed for the docks. They parked near the office of the Deep Sea Charters office. Her dad showed her where the ice and herring were and told her they needed two dozen herring for each customer. The charter company had already set aside sixteen packets of herring as they had eight customers expected for the day.

Jessie went down to the **Jazzer** and dropped off her three sandwiches and candy bars and her extra clothes. She then picked up the two five gallon plastic pails and went back to the office and filled them with ice. She put the packets of herring on top of the ice and began the trip back across the road and down the ramps onto the dock and then on out to the boat. The buckets of ice were heavy and she had to stop a few times to get her breath and then continued. She was determined to do the work and not complain. But her arms felt heavy and they hurt. Still, she arrived on board with everything intact.

It was an odd feeling standing on the quiet boat all by herself. The morning mists made it feel like she was the only person in the world. She could hear noises from some of the other boats as the crews were arriving, but the sound was muted.

"This is the life," she thought to herself. The sunrise was also muted by the fog, but the air was cool, damp and smelled of seaweed and diesel fumes from the boats getting started for the day. Jessie breathed deeply. It was very satisfying. "Well, I can't stand here forever. There's work to be done."

She put the ice into the two ice chests on board and put her sandwiches and candy bars into the smaller ice chest. Then she collected the fishing poles that had been stored in the cabin overnight, and took them out and leaned them against the ship cabin.

She looked around. The **Jazzer** was 43' long and had a level deck which made it easy to move around and help the fishermen. The canopy was white. It was a good boat in good condition and her dad took a lot of pride in keeping it looking good. It was painted white with a green stripe all around it. That was the color combination for her dad's charter fishing company, the Deep Sea Charters. Fishin Fun Charters boats were green with two orange stripes, Big Catch Charter Company boats were blue with a white stripe. All had different combinations. When on the ocean, a person could tell quickly which company was fishing nearby by the colors.

Her dad was coming down the ramp to the dock, walking to the **Jazzer**, calling out to some people and having many call out to him. It was eerie in the fog but everyone was used to it. All of the Deep Sea Charter boats were on Float 8 and they were all friends.

It was oddly quiet but the fog was beginning to lift. Then she saw her dad approaching. He stepped onto deck and asked, "You sure you want to do all this work still?" Jessie was smiling and her eyes gleamed.

"I am sure I can handle this," she answered.

Bob waited and moment and then said, "Jessica. This is a typical man's job and it is a lot of work. But your main job is to make the customers enjoy themselves. If they hook a fish, you be right there with a net in hand to land it. If they lose their bait, you be right there to rebait their hook. You need to watch carefully and when someone calls out 'Fish on,' you be the first one there with a net to help land the fish. You're also there to help the fisherman move up and down the deck trying to land a fish. It's a challenge for the other fishermen to keep fishing when a man is running back and forth trying to land a fish. It's easy for lines to get tangled and you are there to help as much as you can. So, stay alert. You need to talk with them. You need to make sure their experience is a good one. Be cheerful and be interested in them. Keep 'em happy! Keep 'em happy! That make sense to you?"

Jessie nodded. "Sure. I'll talk their heads off."

Captain Martin laughed but he wondered to himself if Jessie could be outgoing enough to be a good deckhand. She was a singularly quiet, observant child. He mentally kicked himself, "I am going to have to think of her as a person, not a child." She was quick to learn but her quietness could hurt her as a deckhand. However, he was sure this was going to be a fun day. It would be interesting to see what "talk their heads off" was going to be like.

"O.K." he said, "Let me get the engine started and then I'll show you how to plug the herring." He went into the cabin and on up to the wheelhouse and started the motor. He glanced at the many dials. All was well.

Jessie put the herring on the cutting board and got a bait knife from the tool box and waited. Bob came over and showed her how to lop the heads off at an angle that left a wedge shape. Jessie took her knife and carefully cut the head off at the angle her dad had showed her. "Why do you cut them off at that angle?" she asked.

"It makes them wriggle in the water like they are alive. That makes them more attractive to the salmon. A blunt straight cut just makes them spin. You cut the plug different ways for different salmon. The silvers like a fast spin and the Chinook like a wobbly spin. You plug about half of these packages. You can fix more as the day goes on if you need them. When you're finished, I'll show you which weights I want on the poles."

"This O.K. with you?" he asked.

"This is so O.K.," Jessie responded.

Bob laughed. For sure, this was definitely going to be an interesting day.

Jessie was busy plugging the bait. She was biting her lip as she concentrated on her work. "I hope I get some tips today. This is gucky work," she thought to herself. It took her a half hour to finish.

When she was finished, Bob showed her where the salmon pins were. These were used to identify which fish belonged to which fisherman as the fish were all put into the large ice chest. A salmon pin is a heavy pin that looks a lot like a safety pin, but it is about three inches long with a number on it. It was inserted into the gill/mouth area to keep the salmon marked with the number assigned to the fisherman who caught it.

"You now need to put a four-ounce sinker on the leaders and get them on the poles so everything is ready for the bait later." He showed her where the sinkers were kept and how to tell which ones were four ounces. She had been on the boat with him before so it wasn't too hard to do. She attached the sinkers to the leaders and then attached the sinkers to the poles. Soon all was ready.

She dug out her first sandwich and ate her breakfast. "I am soooo lucky," she told herself. She was anxious for the first customers to arrive. The day seemed like a dream. It didn't really seem real. "This had better not be a dream," she thought to herself.

It wasn't too long before the first pair of fishermen showed up with coffee cups in hand. "O.K. to come aboard?" they called out.

"Hop on," Captain Martin called back. They came on board and stowed their cooler and rain clothes in the cabin. "Fishin' been any good, Bob?" they inquired.

"Pretty good lately. You've picked a good time to come fishing," Captain Martin responded. The two men were looking at Jessie with a puzzled look on their faces.

"This is my daughter, Jessie. She is going to be our deckhand today," Captain Martin said.

"Gonna use her for bait?" they asked.

Jessie laughed. "At least I am bigger than the fish," she responded.

They all laughed. The taller of the two men said, "Well. It is a good thing that she is bigger than the fish."

The rest of the fishermen showed up two and three at a time. Finally everyone was on board and had signed the sign on sheet. Each customer signed on a numbered line and the line was the number they used for the salmon pins. It was an easy way to keep track of who caught each fish as the day went on.

Captain Martin welcomed all of the fishermen and introduced himself and Jessie. He showed them where the life jackets were stowed. "We have trash containers for all trash," he said. "It is important to not have any trash get into the ocean."

"Cast off," he called to Jessie. She hopped down on the float and untied the lines and left them on the dock and then hopped back onto the boat.

Several of the fishermen were eying Jessie warily when the first two fishermen noticed the glances. "At least she's bigger than the fish," they commented good naturedly. Everyone grinned and hoped for the best.

The day went along quickly. Jessie was a great help to all. She netted the fish well, re-baited their hooks, put the numbered pins in the gills to identify who had caught each fish before it was put onto ice and generally enjoyed herself.

Jessie was talking to one of the fishermen about the salmon he had just caught. Her unabated happiness and constant smile on her first day was contagious and all of the fishermen relaxed and immersed themselves into the sport of fishing. Most got their limit and all went well.

She had just rebaited one of the fishermen lines when she caught her dad looking at her. She looked at him quizzically.

"You're doing a good job, Jessie. The guys all tell me you are doing great."

When Captain Martin finally headed the boat toward the harbor, Jessie cleaned the fish. While she was cleaning the fish, seagulls began to flutter close to her station. She had seen the deckhands do this on an earlier trip so she threw the "innards" up in the air and one of the seagulls nearly always caught it before it hit the water. It was great fun.

One of the men asked if she would fillet his fish. Captain Martin told him Jessie had never filleted fish, but if he would wait until the boat was docked, he would fillet the fish so Jessie could learn how. This worked out just fine.

4

After all of the customers were gone, Bob took the boat to the diesel fuel docks and filled the tank. Then he returned to his slip and showed Jessie where the hose, buckets, soap and scrub brushes were kept. Jessie hooked up the water hose and then took a five gallon bucket and poured liquid soap and bleach into it and filled it with water. She checked the fish cutting board and rinsed it. She then began scrubbing the deck and sides of the boat with the soapy water. She cleaned the exterior sides down to the water line. After the soaping, she took the hose and rinsed everything off.

Captain Martin cleaned out the cabin and made sure there was a good supply of leaders and sinkers for the next day. It took about an hour and a half. When they had everything shipshape, they walked back to the car and drove home.

What a day," Jessie thought to herself. She was tired but she sure was happy. She had chatted with all the customers and had done everything that she thought her dad expected of her. She hoped her dad was satisfied with her work.

Betty had spaghetti for supper that night. She made her own sauce and it was delicious. Jessie had seconds. "My, my. Working on the boat must agree with you," Betty commented. "I suppose you were working too hard for this to help you gain weight."

"This really tastes good to me. You are a super cook, Betty."

Her dad patted his stomach. "For sure, this was a good supper, honey."

He paused and looked at Jessie. "You did very well today." Then he paused again. "Deckhanding is hard work and the day is long. You want to try this again tomorrow?"

Jessie nodded vigorously. "I really like working with the customers and I sure don't mind the long hours."

Bob nodded. "Well, we'll try again tomorrow and then decide. That still ok with you?" Another pause. "You did really well today and I am proud of you."

She made her three cheese sandwiches and got her three candy bars ready for the next day. "I'm going to bed now," she told Barbara and her dad early that evening. "I am pooped." She was asleep before her head hit the pillow.

5

The next day she was a little sore but everything went well. After the customers were gone and she was rinsing off the boat, Bob asked her, "You think you can handle this much work and the long days, every day, for the rest of the summer?"

"Yup," she responded.

"Well, you did a good job today again. But I am still not sure you are physically big or strong enough to do this much work every day. If you decide it is too much, let me know. I'll understand."

She still wanted the job. No problem. She loved deckhanding. However, she asked her Dad if he could let her run into the A-1 Café for a minute on their way home. She popped in the front door and found Harry still in the kitchen. "He puts in long hours too," she thought to herself.

"Harry," she said, "My dad is going to let me deckhand for him for the rest of the summer. If it is OK with you, I'll work my regular nights until you can find someone else to take my place."

He stopped and looked at her. "You're too small to deckhand. It's a man's job, but," he paused, "it pays better than night kitchen work." He grinned. She was too small but he was pretty sure she would be a darned good deck-hand. "I suspect you can do anything you set your mind to," he added

Jessie laughed, "The customers said they were glad I was bigger than the fish."

Harry laughed and returned to his cooking. "Come on in tomorrow night. But that will be all I need. I'm sure Mandy can come in after that."

"Thanks Harry," she replied and hurried back out to the waiting car.

"Is Harry going to be able to find someone to take your job OK," her dad asked.

"Yup. I need to show up tomorrow night and he can manage after that." Jessie paused, "He thinks I am too small. But he also says deckhanding pays better than prep cooking and he thinks I can be a good deckhand. And he says this all in one breath."

Bob laughed. "He's right, you know. If you were five foot eight or nine, it would be a bit better. You need to con-centrate on growing, Jessie." And he laughed again.

6

"Are you fishing today also?" the very pretty woman asked.

Jessie smiled. "No. I get to work. I deckhand for the **Jazzer**. My name is Jessie and Captain Martin is my father."

"Well, I am glad you are here. My name is Harriet and I was worried that I might be the only woman on board for the whole day," she responded smiling.

The rest of the guests showed up in two and threes. They all signed the sign-up sheet and soon they were on their way. There was a light wind, a few clouds and the ocean was choppy. The morning mists cleared away to a cool sunshine between the clouds.

The fishing was slow for the first couple of hours, so Captain Martin moved the boat and found a better spot.

"Tell the customer to drop their lines about 30 feet. That is about 10 arm lengths."

Jessie told everyone what the Captain recommended. So, people were gradually catching some fish.

"Jessie wandered back to the wheel house, "How do you know where to fish?" she asked.

Bob filled his pipe again. "Fish can see forward and up ... but not down. So, you need the bait in front of and above to attract them. To find where the salmon are, you look for clues like those whale birds feeding on the ocean. Also, there are salmon rips – a line of different colors of water that show where two different currents collide. This traps plankton and small fish that salmon feed on. Sometime the salmon themselves are jumping or "finning" while feeding on the surface. They swim deeper on sunny days and come closer to the surface on cloudy days. Together with the fish finder, you can learn about where they would be. Experienced captains can help a lot."

He looked at Jessie with a smile, "You pay attention to everything."

Almost all had caught at least one and several had hooked two. The boat moved slowly. The fish finder showed the salmon were there. Then, one of the fishermen had reeled in a salmon almost to the boat. Jessie had a net and was alongside of him ready to net the fish.

The salmon was finally being drug on its side in the water for Jessie to net when a dark flash came along and hit the salmon and was gone. Jessie netted the salmon and was surprised to see that half of it was gone.

"Dad," she called. "What's going on here?"

"Shark," one of the fishermen called out.

Jessie's dad came out of the cabin and nodded his head. "Yeah. Shark will do that. It happens. Just keep on fishing," and he ducked back into the cabin.

Jessie was amazed at the calm tones of the fisherman and her father. "Shark. Like man eaters?" she wondered to herself. Then in the blinking of an eye, one of the fishermen managed to get a shark up onto the deck. It flipped and squirmed and everyone backed away from it, as it was pretty good sized.

Jessie sidled over to another spot on the deck and the shark watched her move. It turned its head and followed her with its eyes. Jessie was totally startled as she had never seen a fish actually look at something. Captain Martin arrived and handed a gaff to Jessie and then began to try to stab the fish with his own gaff.

"Back away, people," he called. "We don't want anyone to get bit."

He swung his gaff, which was about the size of a baseball bat that had a large curved hook protruding from the end. Jessie tried to sink her gaff into the shark but found the shark was very squirmy ... much like an eel. Keeping away from the teeth, they managed, with a good deal of effort, to snag the shark and throw it back into the ocean.

"Not a good fish to have on board," her dad said as he went back into the cabin.

"Especially not good if they get big enough to be able to eat people," Jessie thought to herself.

She hurried around to get all of the fishermen in place with good bait. They were pretty excited about the episode.

"Bet that shark is too sore to steal any more of our salmon," one of them said.

Jessie wondered to herself about the likeness to an eel that that shark had displayed. None of the fish they were used to catching were anything like that shark. Having the thing follow her with its eyes had unnerved her a bit. That shark was surely a different kind of fish.

Harriet caught her eye. Jessie went over. "You have an unusual job," Harriet said. "I've never seen anyone so calm about picking up a shark and throwing it back into the water."

Jessie smiled. "Well, my Dad did most of the work. I just helped a bit. That shark was quite a fish, don't you think?"

Harriet smiled and shrugged. "I wish I had remembered my camera. Telling stories about our vacation will sure include the one about the girl who catches sharks."

7

Towards the end of that first summer, there came a day when the weather was too rough to take out the boat, so the trip was canceled and Jessie had a rainy, windy day to herself. Bob offered to take her to Seattle if she wanted to do some shopping for school clothes. He needed to go for some business and figured she could tag along if she wanted.

She had earned enough money to buy most of her own clothes and would still have quite a bit left over. A quick call to her Mom and a plan was hatched that Bob would take her to Seattle and her mom would go with her shopping. Then, come early evening, Bob would bring her back to Westport.

"Far out," Jessie commented. The trip to Seattle would be three hours driving up and three hours back, so it would be a long day. She did not like shopping, but she had grown some over the summer and was about eight pounds heavier.

So, new clothes would be nice. She was immensely proud to be purchasing her own clothes. "I could make enough money to support myself if I was not in school," she thought to herself.

Bob dropped her off at her Mom's house and said he would be back between seven and eight.

"Thanks, dad," Jessie responded. "See you then."She started up the sidewalk and her mom, Laura, came out the front door. She caught Jessie up in a big hug. Jessie's mom was dressed in a neatly tailored cream colored suit. She was very trim and had an elegant air about her.

Jessie looked at her. She was so different from the women she met on the fishing boats. Almost all of the women who came fishing were very casual in their blue jeans, tops and tennies. Jessie nodded. This was definitely her mother, looking like she had stepped out of a fashion magazine. Her high heels matched her suit color and looked very comfortable.

"You look great, Jess. I was afraid you would be skin and bones deckhanding every day but you look like you are thriving!" she said.

"Well, if gaining weight is thriving, then I'm thriving," Jessie laughed. "I definitely need some new clothes. You look great, too, Mom."

Her mom smiled, "You are tan and looking very fit. You enjoying your job?"

Jessie nodded vigorously.

"Well," Laura continued, "I can see why we're looking for new clothes. You're filling out nicely, young lady."

They went to a big department store first and began browsing. Jessie found a coat she really liked and several pairs of shoes. Then they found a mall and looked some more. It felt strange being in the bright lights with all the color and commotion. After buying several pairs of jeans that fit nicely and several blouses and sweaters she asked, "This is enough to get me started, don't you think?" she asked her mother.

"Sure. These are great. Let's go to the food court and find something to eat. I am sure you are starving," her mom replied

While she was munching on a taco, Jessie mentioned to her mom that she could make enough money to support herself, if she didn't have to go to school.

Her mom smiled. "Jessica, it is astounding how much money you are making. I doubt if there is any other girl making as much as you do. But being a seafaring gypsy for the rest of your life is another thing. Life is sixty or seventy years long and deckhanding is tough. If you don't mind the work, good for you. However, if you haven't already, before you make it your career of choice, talk to your dad."

When Captain Martin picked her up and they had driven for about an hour, Jessie said to her dad, "I am kind of thinking about becoming a full-time deckhand and not going back to school. What do you think?"

Her dad gave a short laugh and said, "How many reasons do you want me to give you about staying in school until you graduate? Five, ten, a hundred? How many reasons are there for dropping out early? One? Maybe. One and a half?" He paused, found his pipe and, with a great deal of ceremony, filled it, lit it and finally took a long pull on it. "Seriously, Jessie. You need to play the odds and odds are, you will do better over a lifetime if you finish high school. You should consider college for the same reasons ... better odds over a lifetime."

There was a long silence while Jessie thought about this. "I make pretty good money deckhanding. I could do it," she said, voicing her thoughts. "If I could work for a full season instead of only summer vacation and weekends, I could manage through the winter. I could maybe get a captain's license eventually and run a charter boat like you do. I might even buy my own boat one day."

She paused a moment, shrugged her shoulders, and then continued, "It is a career that does not need a college degree for sure and probably not even require a high school diploma."

Captain Martin nodded in agreement. "However, like I said, having a diploma is playing with the best odds of a successful life and/or career."

There was another silence, then he continued. "Wanting to be your own person and to be independent is very normal for kids your age. And you're right, it could be possible to live on the money earned during salmon season. But, try thinking about the long term effects of this decision."

He chuckled again, "And, please, please decide to finish high school. Your mother would have my hide if I provided you a way to become independent and not finish school. We both want you to go to college, but at this stage, we might settle for high school."

Jessie was still caught up in her dream of being on her own and did not respond.

"I think you are smart enough to do the right thing. But, I am going to have to tell you, Jessie, that you are a kick to watch go by." Her dad was chuckling to himself. These serious conversations with Jessie were entertaining as he knew her well enough to know she would finish high school and get her diploma one way or another. She had an aptitude for working with people and loved being on the ocean. He was confident she would be just fine.

Jessie loved thinking of the "what ifs" if she quit school and became a "sea gypsy" as her mother put it. It would be such an adventure but she did love playing her cello with the Youth Symphony and her classes, at least some of them, were quite interesting. And, she thought, Chuck Hammond was an awfully cute boy who was paired with her for Chemistry Lab experiments.

Chuck was also taking an Intro to Physics class which he was really into. One time, he told Jenny about it while they were assembling the chemistry lab assignments. "Jess. Newtonian mechanics are really really basic. Today, Mr. Henry was demonstrating the way motion transports energy but not matter..." He continued recounting the physics lesson while he was heating a glass tube for the lab assignment.

Jessie had tuned him out. He was cute and easy going but he was sure into that physics stuff.

8

Jessie was surviving her junior year in high school. She had deckhanded all last summer for her dad and had worked through the fall weekends until the season had closed. Now is was May and she was scheduled for deckhanding again on weekends.

As was her custom each day, she went to work with three cheese sandwiches and three Three Musketeer candy bars. One sandwich was eaten early in the day after she had the bait and poles ready for fishing and the other two sandwiches were eaten around noon. The candy bars were snacks for when she felt like eating them.

She wore her work boots, a light cotton shirt under a sweater which was under a heavy sweater for cooler, rainy days. On warmer, sunny days she wore a baseball style cap, tennies and dark glasses. She hadn't grown any taller but was about 105 pounds now and had decided she was not going to be a tall woman. Her richly colored chestnut hair was still in braids and was tucked through the back of the cap.

The first weekend of salmon fishing was fully booked. The morning fog and light rain made the deck and railings slick. Today Jessie had on her rain slicker and sou'wester together with her work shoes. It was a very typical morning for Westport as the fog-bank did not burn off until midmorning. When the light rain stopped, Jessie breathed deeply, enjoying the moisture. Being on the ocean was pleasant and she felt at home on the boat.

"At least I'm bigger than the fish," she laughed to herself. She had gotten a big kick out of that description from the men on her first day. They were some of the people who fished with Captain Martin every year, so she figured she would see them again this spring.

The twelve customers booked for that day included two women. This was good as it was easier in some ways than being the only female on board. The teasing about being dinky AND a girl was fun in a way, but she knew it would not be so intense with women along.

Captain Martin was coming down the ramp to the float. People, unseen in the fog, called out to him as he came toward the **Jazzer**.

"You about ready for our guests?" he asked her as he stepped onto the deck.

"Yup," Jessie answered. She was already eating her first sandwich in the cabin. It did not seem so cold and damp with the water heating for the coffee and cocoa.

"Our starting time tomorrow is going to be five in the morning. The bar should be ok today but tomorrow the low tide will cause the bar to be too dangerous so we need to leave earlier to avoid it. Our customers have all been told of the earlier time and there is no problem for any of them," he said.

Jessie thought back to the previous summer when her dad had explained the problems with the mouth of the harbor. He had stuck his hand up with the fingers spread, "My wrist is the bar and mouth of the harbor. My fingers are the rivers that empty into Grays Harbor. After a big rain and the rivers are running full and the tide is really really low, the strong current from the rivers mix with the ocean's low tide at the mouth, and they basically mix and eddy and have no particular direction. The mouth of the harbor is narrow and the currents come from both sides, from behind, from ahead and it is very difficult to take a boat through them. It is very dangerous. About one and a half hours before low tide is the roughest."

"If we leave about five tomorrow, we'll miss the bad time," he added

Just then, out of the fog, came four of their fishermen. "Hey! Skipper! You needing some suckers to take fishing today?"

Bob laughed. "That's the best kind of fisherman. Come on board! But watch out for the steps and the deck. The fog has made them a bit slick."

The foursome stepped onto the deck and headed for the cabin to stow their cooler. They were wearing rain-gear.

"Be sure and sign the sign-up sheet," Jessie said. "There's hot water for coffee or tea if you want some." The sign-up sheet had numbered lines to sign. The numbers gave each guest his number so when he caught a salmon, a numbered fish pin would be put in its gills to identify it from the other salmon in the fish box.

The rest of the guests showed up. Jessie noticed some were first timers and she told them about the sign-up sheet. If they signed up on line nine, then nine was the number given to their salmon. Everyone's salmon was labeled with their number to keep track of who caught what.

Captain Martin then introduced himself and Jessie and gave his welcoming speech. He showed everyone the location of the life vests and emphasized that NO trash ever went overboard. He then began his normal two knots an hour exit from the marina. Jessie had heard this speech every day and could recite it from memory.

As soon as they cleared the marina, the boat picked up speed and was soon at the mouth of the harbor. After they cleared the harbor and were on the ocean, the boat went to full speed. The three hundred and fifty salmon fishing boats were all busy. Some had left earlier but all had to be very alert with the fog and narrow part of the harbor as they headed out. It was a colorful and exciting time.

The various captains from Deep Sea Charters Company talked to each other on channel 39 on the VHF radios. Each company had a different channel so the different charter companies would not have to talk over each other. Channel 16 was used exclusively for emergencies and the Coast Guard monitored it.

The Deep Sea Charter captains talked until one of them started having bites. He gave his location to the others and they all came to the area. Collectively, it was an efficient way to find where the salmon were biting.

The morning mist had lifted and it was sunny and warm. The fishing was good and the customer were calling out "Fish On!" when they had hooked a fish. Jessie was very busy helping the fishermen net the salmon.

By that afternoon, the fishing was slowing and, when Jenny was chatting with a customer, he asked her, "Jessie, what is there to do in Westport? We have all day tomorrow and I wondered what would be interesting to see."

Jessie nodded. "I really like seeing the lighthouse. They let you go up to the top and the view is amazing. The lens is astounding too."

She paused. "The museum is interesting. There is always good music at various places and, of course, shell hunting along the beaches is good. It's fun to take a picnic to the beach and build a fire."

He smiled. "Thanks. We'll be sure and see it all if we can."

9

Once the day was over and all was ready for the next day, Captain Martin told Jessie he wanted to stop by Kevin's boat for a few minutes.

"You want me to go to the car and wait or go with you?" she asked

"Come along if you wish. We're just going to talk about this new proposal for taking the limit from three to two fish," he replied.

They came to Kevin's boat and stepped onto the deck. Kevin's deckhand had already left but Kevin was waiting in the cabin with a bottle of beer in this hand.

"Want a beer?" he asked Bob.

"Do fish swim?" Bob replied.

Jessie helped herself to cocoa. The tea kettle still had some hot water and she knew where the cocoa mix was.

"You've heard about changing the limit?" Bob asked Kevin.

"Yeah. I've also heard they are thinking about shortening the season also," Kevin responded.

He stopped and rubbed his eyes. He was tired after a long day and he was speaking very deliberately. "You figure an average of eight fishermen per boat and three hundred and fifty boats. That makes almost three thousand fishermen getting two or three salmon a day. It seems like a huge number but yet the salmon are still teeming out there. It is amazing but I don't think their concern about the salmon numbers is correct. There are plenty of salmon."

Bob was nodding in agreement. "I guess they're putting lower limits on the commercial fishing boats, too," Bob said. "But I am thinking this could put a big damper on our business, if it happens."

Kevin nodded his head. "There's not a thing we can do about it. And I think it will kill our industry."

Both men were silent for a moment and they then started chatting about the day's catch. After his beer was gone, Bob stood up and said, "Thanks for the beer." He turned to Jessie. "We better head for home," and he motioned for her to start heading for the door. Jessie put her paper cocoa cup and Bob's empty beer bottle in the trash and started out.

Once they were in the car, Jessie asked her Dad, "What kind of trouble will come from changing the limit and season length?"

Bob sighed and blew the air through his nostrils like a charging bull. He was exasperated and it showed. "The owners of these boats have paid a whole lot of money for them and they need to make pretty good money to make their payments and keep them in good repair. If the demand for fishing drops, their income will drop and it is hard to make payment with no money. If the limit drops from three to two salmon, fewer people will want to fish. The fishing experience will be mostly for enjoyment, not as a way to get salmon a little cheaper than buying them in a grocery store. Like we say, if you want a guarantee, go to the grocery store but if you want a great day on the ocean, come fishing with us."

He paused. His brow was furrowed as he frowned. "We just have to hope the Fisheries people will let the recreational fishermen keep three and try to limit the commercial fishermen. The Fisheries people think the salmon numbers are getting too low and that we are overfishing them."

He added, "However, I think that they will lower the limit and shorten the season from May to September. There's a lot of people worried about this. We just have to wait and see. Wait and see."

10

The next morning again was foggy, damp and cool. It was also darker because of the earlier hour. Jessie was ready for the customers and was having her first cup of hot chocolate of the day when her dad came on board to start the engines.

People were again appearing out of the fog. The feeling, as usual, was happy and the anticipation of catching salmon made for big smiles from the group. All of them had fished with Captain Martin before so there were lots of jokes.

"This is about like Disneyland sometimes," Jessie thought to herself. "Not a bad way to make a living, I'd say."

The **Jazzer** came to the mouth of the harbor in the mist but Captain Martin took the **Jazzer** through it with little trouble. They hit the open ocean and found a good fishing spot within the hour.

The day went normally, and after a good day fishing and the customers were gone, she was mopping the sides of the boat and the floor when she asked her dad. "There is a first aid course being given in Westport next week. Do you think it would be a good thing for me to attend?"

Bob stopped for just about a half of a second. "It would be a really great thing for you to do," he answered

That evening she went down to the Sugarloaf. They had live music and she enjoyed listening. She spotted Jason, one of the deckhands for another Deep Sea Charter boat. He was sitting in a corner booth with two other deck hands. She joined them and ordered a coke. Although she was only seventeen, the Sugarloaf people knew her and said nothing.

"Did you guys have good fishing today? Any trouble with the bar?" she asked Jason.

"A couple of them limited, but most just caught two. A little on the slow side and the bar was ok. That is sure an interesting problem when it occurs. You hear stories about boats wrecking sometimes when they are not prepared for it," he answered. "How did you guys do?"

"About the same." She listened to the reggae style music. "Far out," she commented.

Jason grinned. "You know old Mike and Hank here, don't you, Jess?" he asked.

She nodded.

"You want to dance, Jessie" Mike asked.

"Nope," she replied. "Listening is enough for me."

"I took a bath and probably don't smell like fish, if that is your problem," he quickly returned.

Jessie ignored the three guys exchanging banter. The music was loud and she could not hear half of what was being said but she nodded and smiled. It was easygoing and typical of the deckhands when they saw each other. All of the deckhands for Deep Sea Charters knew each other as they had visited on the occasions when they were docking about the same time or when they were carrying ice and herring in the morning.

"Well, here's to the best charter company in Westport," Hank said, lifting his beer bottle in salute.

"Float 8 is the best," chimed in Jason.

Jessie lifted her coke glass and nodded her head.

"I'm going to take the first aid course next week," she announced during a break in the music. "Any of you guys going to sign up for it?

Jason nodded yes but the rest just shrugged.

That next week Jessie had been home, showered, grabbed a sandwich for supper by 5:30 and was on her way to the fire station. The course hours were from six until ten and were specifically chosen to accommodate the fishing fleet employees.

Jason was already there when she arrived and when she appeared at the door, he motioned to the chair next to him. She nodded and went to the registration table and started to fill in an application.

"You need to be sixteen to take this course," the registrar told her.

"I am seventeen," she retorted.

He smiled. "O.K. then. No problem," he replied. "I will need some kind of picture ID and twenty dollars," he added.

Jessie got out her driver's license and the money and handed them to him. He nodded and soon the paper work was finished.

She walked over to Jason and sat in the chair he had been saving for her. "That guy needed to see a picture ID for me before he would let me register," Jessie groused.

Jason snorted to himself and then laughed out loud. "For Pete's sake, Jessie. It's not his fault that you look like you are twelve," and he continued laughing to himself.

Jessie looked at him and scowled. "Now I know why I dislike you so much," she said and then broke out laughing also.

The instructor soon asked everyone to quiet down. There were about twenty people taking the course. Most of them looked like deckhands and several were from the commercial salmon fishing boats and there was one older guy who looked vaguely familiar to Jenny. She knew he lived in Westport but did not really know him.

A young-looking fireman stood in front and announced. "This is a general first aid course," and began handing out the Red Cross First Aid Manual to everyone. "There will be a twenty minute break at eight. Same thing tomorrow night." He was smiling and seemed to be pretty relaxed. Jessie realized she was a little tense. "I wonder what is making me a little up tight?" she thought to herself. "Being the only woman here is normal for me. Not sure what else I might be feeling." However, she soon also relaxed as the class began.

"This is a standard course and not specific to the fishing industry. You should pay attention to all of the information because you may need to know these things if you come upon an automobile wreck with injuries, for example."

"We'll begin by showing you a good first aid kit and demonstrating how to use the contents."

"Does anyone know what a butterfly bandage is and what it is designed to do?"

Two hands went up and the session began.

The next night they learned resuscitation on ResusciAnnie ... the dummy designed for them to learn how to breathe for someone and how to do chest compressions.

Jessie was amazed at all she had learned. It was totally useful information and she was really proud of her First Aid Card. Also, it tickled her to make a couple of suggestions for the First Aid Kit on the boat.

11

Graduation had been exciting but Jessie's heart was out on the ocean and she was anxious to get back to Westport. She knew her parents were disappointed that she was not making plans to go on to college. But the cool, clean air, the customers enjoying themselves, the whole experience kept her charmed. She knew she would never tire of salmon fishing.

Jessie's mom was helping her pack the last things in her room in preparation for another summer in Westport.

"Do you think you might want to do something different in a few years? Deckhanding seems like a dead end type of career. Maybe in a year or so, you could go to college," her mom added.

Jessie thought for a minute. "Mom. It is hard to describe the satisfaction I get from being with the customers every day. It is a joy. I love being on the ocean."

She stopped. Then haltingly she continued, "If I want to consider it, I could decide to get a Captain's license. I could make enough money to eventually buy my own boat and make a lifetime career. Or just be a captain. They make enough money in one season to last through the winter. It is a living wage. Not a dead end job."

"Honey, there are no women salmon boat captains now. Maybe people will not pay money to have a woman captain for their fishing day. Is there a fatal flaw somewhere in your idea?"

Jessie was smiling to herself by now. "I think it is that way because no woman has tried."

She gave her mom a big smile. "I can be a trend setter or something. That sound good to you?"

Another pause.

"Actually, staying on as a deckhand is nearly a good living wage. I don't have to do much to earn my way from year to year." Jessie was glad her mother did not know of the expected trouble within the industry if the limit was lowered and/or the season was shortened.

Her mom shrugged her shoulders and gave Jessie a hug. "Well, if there is anyone who can make this plan work, it is you, Jessica, and your room will be ready any time you want to come home. I will miss you, you know." Her Mom smiled to herself. Jessie was grown up but she was still small. "I hope you stay tough enough to handle your job," she added.

Her Mom drove her to the bus station. "You call from time to time and let me know if you still think you're on a summer vacation instead of a job. O.K.?" her mom said as she helped her get her three suitcases into the depot.

"Sure," Jessie said. "Thanks for everything. Now I am off to my big adventure," and she smiled at her mother and gave her a hug.

Jessie went to the ticket window and purchased her ticket to Aberdeen. The bus was about ready to leave, so she and her mom took her luggage to the bus where the driver deposited it in the basement of the bus. Jessie gave her mother another hug and got onto the bus. It had the usual semi-dusty smell all buses had. She walked down the aisle and found a seat, put her coat and umbrella on the seat and slid in beside them and then looked out the window.

The bus was closing its doors and ready to roll. Jessie waved goodbye to her mom. Such a strange feeling. Old enough now to be her own person. She felt anxious, unsure and elated all at the same time.

The bus arrived in Aberdeen three hours later and her dad was there waiting for her.

"Hello the bus," he called as she came down the steps.

"Hello the parent," she responded.

He gave her a quick hug and went to the side of the bus to retrieve her luggage. Jessie carried one suitcase and he got the other two.

"You ready for work tomorrow?" he asked.

"Yup. For sure," she said. "Dad, I think I should get an apartment or something. I'm through school and need to be taking care of myself."

Bob smiled. This was a daughter definitely growing up. "There's no hurry, honey," he said. "Why don't you just give us some money to cover your food costs. Ask Betty about that. She and I like having you around and it is sure nice to have help with Sam." He stopped and glanced at her. It was hard to imagine that this very small daughter could be old enough to live on her own.

The Fisheries did change the salmon limit from three to two and had changed the starting date to May 15th also. The general level of griping and frustration among the charter companies was rising. Letters to the editor and phone calls to Olympia fell on deaf ears. The Fisheries people were convinced that the salmon population was dropping too fast. Rivers being dammed had kept thousands of fish from being able to return to their spawning grounds and the once huge number of fish was dropping. They felt the salmon population was in trouble.

The whole summer changed. Some of the guest fishermen decided the cost of fishing with the charter companies was too expensive for just two fish and did not return. Occasionally, there were so few people signed up to fish that two of the boats would have to combine their customers. This left one captain and his deckhands not working. More often than not, one of the captains would deckhand for the other. This left the brunt of the customer loss on the deckhands. In any case, there was less money to be made.

Bob Martin had had mostly full boats and had not coupled with another boat to get a full load. But there were lots of times he was short one or two fishermen. Bob had enough repeat business to continue to do well. Believing his approach to making sure the customers were happy and the lighthearted atmosphere on the boat was what kept people coming back worked well. The boats whose skippers were gruff or sarcastic were the first to start having trouble with not having enough customers to make it worthwhile to take the boat out on the ocean.

Jessie's summer routine stayed much the same as it had been the previous two summers and she was happy.

"Hey, Jess," one of the customers called out. "You going to sneak a couple of extra fish into my pocket?"

"Oh, sure thing," she retorted. "Would three be better?"

The salmon were usually at least 12-14 pounds clear up to forty plus later in the season, so this was definitely a joke and the customers laughed. The day went well and, as usual, they were happy and joking and having just plain fun. Captain Martin told Jessie he would have to leave early so she would have to do all the cleaning and lock up.

"No problem," she said cheerfully.

The daily cleanup took longer but she kind of enjoyed it. It was different to do the scrubbing and hosing with no one else around and it was different to clean the cabin. She put the poles in the cabin and locked the door for the night. When all was shipshape, she stepped onto the float and started home when she heard Jason, "Hey, Jess Jess. You have some time?"

"Sure," she said and slowed down until he caught up with her.

"I have such a deal for you," he started.

She smiled. "He sure gets to the point in a hurry," she thought to herself.

He continued, "I am going back east this spring and won't be deckhanding this year. If I go now instead of this fall, I can have a really good part time job to help with college expenses. So, I have this really top notch first class really really small trailer to sell and you, newly hatched as you are, came to mind." He grinned at her. They had arrived at the main street off the harbor.

There were lots of people around. Some were tourists. Some were families of the fishermen out on the boats. There were five hundred or so people working on the boats. All together there were several thousand people each day. The restaurants, gift shops, charter companies were all full of people. It was a busy, hustling street. It was a colorful, noisy place to be. The stores and restaurants were all painted bright colors and if a person turned around and faced the harbor, the boats were all painted bright colors also. Their various shapes, flags on deck and hundreds and hundreds of masts, outriggers and antennae made for an intriguing sight.

The commercial fishermen, with their much bigger boats, were delivering their catch to the wholesale companies. So, the fresh fish businesses were busy as were the canneries. "Just like Disneyland," though Jessie to herself again.

It was an impressive sight. Westport. The Salmon Capitol of the World was a good name for all of the activity.

"You think this might be a good idea for you?" he asked after they had taken in the sight for a few minutes.

"I have to talk with my dad to see what he thinks," Jessie responded. "It might work. But I might need a car before I need to buy a trailer."

He laughed. "I think you might be right about that. I'll talk to Jared. He's talking about finding a place to stay."

"When are you leaving?" she asked.

"Well, I hope you won't miss me too much," and he grinned. "I should be leaving within the week."

Jessie smiled. These deck hands were all like older brothers to her. They were pretty protective.

"Thanks for thinking of me for the trailer," Jessie said.

He punched her in the shoulder and then gave her an awkward hug. "I hope you do well," he said. "And if I were you, I would not get all worked up about becoming a captain.

Jessie flushed. She had mentioned her pipe dream to her buddies and they were not much in favor of it. "Who would hire you?" they asked. They sure didn't pussy foot around in giving their opinions. "With friends like you, who needs enemies?" she asked them,

12

Jessie returned to the car. Bob was not there but was just a step or two behind her. "Good timing," he said. "Thanks for waiting around for me."

They got into the car and started home. After a mile or so, Bob said, "Jess, I've talked to Betty about this, but I am going to go back my old job of tugboating. I'll stay through this season but you will need to start thinking about who could use you as a deckhand. Kevin might or possibly Jack. Check with them, if you want to continue deckhanding, that is."

Jessie was surprised. She had not thought her dad would quit salmon fishing. She was not sure what to say. "Why are you going back to tugboating, Dad?" she asked.

"The pay is good and it is year 'round work, which will be a lot easier on me and Betty. These winters needing to find something to do are getting a little old. I am thinking you can find a job on another boat. You are known for being a good deckhand."

"Are you going to stay in Westport or move somewhere else?" she asked.

"We're going to stay in Westport. We like it here. And you are definitely welcome to continue staying with us. I am thinking if you ask around about deckhanding on another boat, the sooner the better. I can give notice to the owner of the **Jazzer** anytime."

"I guess getting out of this business now makes sense with all the new rules and restrictions," she commented.

"I don't want to discourage you from staying with the salmon fishing business but you are right. There will be fewer and fewer boats going out and that means a lot less jobs. Jessie, it is absolutely a happy way to make a living but its longterm prospects are not good," he responded. "You might reconsider going to college this fall."

"No. Thanks though, but I am going to stick with it, if Kevin or Carl can use me."

Jessie was rubbing her forehead and had one eye closed.

"If there comes a day when I cannot find a job deckhanding," she said slowly. "I guess I could think about college or look somewhere else for work. But I want to do this for as long as I can."

Bob smiled to himself. Jessie definitely had the bug for wanting to work on the ocean. "Do you suppose this business of needing to work on the ocean is contagious ... or maybe just in our genes?" he asked.

Jessie laughed. "Jason just asked me if I wanted to buy his little trailer because he is not going to work this summer. Maybe Kevin could use me. I should at least ask. The **WaterDancer** is a good boat."

"Don't feel like I am kicking you out. There's time to make a move. No real hurry. But I think you are right, Kelly is a good captain to work for," Bob responded. "You want me to ask him or do you want to ask him?"

"I'll see what he thinks tomorrow."

They arrived home and Bob took a quick bath. Jessie did the same in the second bath and they were both presentable in time for supper. Betty had fixed pork chops, gravy, mashed potatoes, broccoli, a small salad and macaroni and cheese. The mac and cheese was mostly for Sam, who preferred them to almost any other food.

Jessie looked at Sam and remembered him from two summers ago. It Took a while for Sam to be admitted to the dining room table, as he threw most of his food off of the tray of his high chair for a long time. He finally settled into eating most of it, finger food style. Today, at three, he used a spoon pretty well, but still preferred finger food. He had a knack of making everyone laugh at his antics. Bob and Jenny were usually famished from working a long day, with just sandwiches to eat. So, watching Sam learn to eat and talk was a fun occupation for supper time. He still called Jessie "Gessie" as he still had troubles with the J sound. He sure had a knack to making people smile.

.

13

After getting the boat in good order the next day, Jessie hurried over to Kevin's boat, hoping to catch him still there. He was checking the oil for an engine when she got there.

"Kevin. Dad wants to go back to tugboat work. Would you consider using me for a deckhand next year?"

He screwed the oil cap back on and looked at her.

"Hello, to you too."

He paused again, grinning. Jessie was obviously anxious about this.

"I knew your dad was considering this move, so it is no surprise."

He paused again, looking at her. "I will be more than happy to have you deckhand for me next spring. You are a very good deck hand. I might be able to use you this fall also, if, whoever I hire to replace Jason, can't work week-ends. Would that work out for you too?"

"That sounds really good. Ummmm. Hello to you."

They both laughed. Jessie looked at her shoes for a moment. Then responded, "I'm sorry Jason is calling it quits. He's a really fun guy."

"See you around."

Jessie found her dad at the car. "Kevin says he can use me next summer."

Bob nodded. "O.K. I'll finish out this season. That'll work out well for giving plenty of notice."

After dinner that night, Jessie went and sat in her usual chair. Sam made a beeline for her lap. He clambered up and put his face squarely in from of hers, about four inches away. "You want some attention, Sam?" she asked him. "Nothing too subtle about you, for sure."

She cuddled him and he beamed. She put him down and went into the kitchen to make the sandwiches for the next day. She was thinking about working for Kevin the next season and thought about getting a car. "Dad," she asked, "do you have any notions about cars? I need to start thinking about getting one for myself."

"I am assuming, you are thinking about a used car. What about a Volkswagen? They get good mileage and are about your size.

Jessie laughed. "I am thinking I need a big car. The bigger the better."

Bob smiled and shook his head. "There is no guessing

what you are thinking ... the bigger the better, huh? Well, try for an '88. That would probably be big enough. We'll get Jimson to look at the engine when you find something. He can help you find one in decent shape."

"An '88?" Jessie tucked her chin back and looked puzzled.

"It's a big car. An Oldsmobile Super '88. You'll like it." He stopped and looked at his feet and then he looked back at Jessie. He was laughing to himself. "It's a muscle car. Right up your alley."

Jessie grinned at him. "How do I start looking?" she asked.

He paused, thinking. "Ask around, look in the news-paper, go to car dealers in Aberdeen or Olympia. Take your time." He stopped again, brows furrowed, "It's easy to get a car with problems when you are in the used car market, so taking plenty of time looking at them helps."

Jessie was standing there looking at him with a puzzled look on her face. He laughed to himself. She was probably expecting him to find one for her. But, she was becoming an adult and needed to learn how to shop for cars.

"When you find one or two that you like, I'll help you get them checked out."

Jessie nodded. It was going to be tough to find time to shop being as how they worked seven days a week.

"Maybe I should start looking when the season is over," she commented.

"Sounds like a good plan to me," her dad responded.

"Could I borrow the pickup for a while tonight? I want to find the guys to chat for a bit."

"No problem. Help yourself," Bob answered.

Jessie was sitting with several of the other Lucky Charter deckhands, having a coke and was just generally listening to the talk. With Jason gone, it was a little sad for her, but Blake was doing a pretty good job of being funny.

"Have you guys ever heard of an '88?" she asked.

They collectively looked at her for a moment. "If you're talking about a car, yes." They had almost spoken in unison. "One of my uncles has one and they are hot," Hank added.

Blake was still looking at her closely. "You have a friend getting one or something?"

Jessie shrugged. "My dad thinks it might be a good car for me."

Again, they collectively looked at her.

Blake finally spoke. "Jessie. An '88 is way too big of a car for you. You'll have problems reaching the brakes. You'll probably have problems seeing over the dashboard." He paused again.

Jessie shrugged again and took a sip of her coke.

"Well, I want a big car."

Blake shook his head and turned to Jim. "Did you have a good day today?" he asked

Jim didn't answer as he was paying close attention to a girl who was sitting three tables over. Blake looked at Jim.

"Hello, wall," he said and turned his gaze to the wall. Everyone laughed at the reference to the Smothers Brothers. Jim returned his attention to his table and found everyone looking at him, laughing.

"What?" he asked, which only made everyone laugh harder.

A tall, blond girl with tanned skin and a cheerful smile came over and said, "You are a rowdy bunch! Mind if I sit with you?"

Everyone skooched over and made room and she sat.

"I'm Susie," she volunteered.

"Ah, I'm Blake. He pointed at each person at the table. This is Jim, Dennis, our mute is Jessie, Boris and Lenny. We're with Deep Sea Charters,"

He was grinning from ear to ear.

Jessie huffed up in fun. "Mute!" she said. She looked at Susie, "With friends like these, who needs enemies? I work as a deckhand for my dad on the **Jazzer**."

"Oh," Susie replied, "I had heard there was another girl deckhanding. We are a rare breed, you know. I deckhand on the **African Queen**."

"I haven't heard of that one," Lenny said.

Susie roared. "Bad joke," she said dabbing at her eyes, I don't work on the **Titanic** either. I work for Bob Jay on the **Fish Finder**."

Jessie liked Susie. She was calm and funny at the same

time. "You been deckhanding for very long?" she asked.

"This is my first year in Westport. I worked a few years in Port Angeles, then my family moved here. I was lucky to find a job here too. A lot of captains don't hire girls."

Lenny stood and backed away from the table. "It was nice meeting you, Susie, but I need to split now. Come sit with us anytime. See you guys," and he wormed his way through the crowd to the door.

"You planning on deckhanding until you're eighty?" Susie asked Jessie.

"Nope," Jessie smiled. There was a long pause and Jessie realized that Susie really wanted to hear what she thought about long term deckhanding. "I like salmon fishing with the tourists. It is a fun job. And maybe someday I could captain a boat also."

Susie nodded. She had tilted her head and her mouth was skewed as she thought. "However, it might be kind of tough finding a boat to captain when so many captains don't even like hiring a girl. I have no idea what the owners would think."

Jessie smiled. "Actually, I am thinking about having my hours validated and when I get enough, taking the test."

"Sounds good to me. I am all for it," Susie responded.

Blake heard this exchange frowning. "Yippy skippy," he said sarcastically. "Jess, you are wasting your time .... And a lot of other people's time also. Even if you do get your hours together and get a captain's license. No one will hire a woman to captain their boats. They have too much money involved."

He looked straight at Jessie. He liked her and knew she did a really good job deckhanding. He and the other Lucky Charter deckhands were proud of her and considered her a younger sister. He really did not want to see her wasting her time or getting her hopes up.

"Back east," he continued, "They consider it bad luck to have a woman on board. You don't see it so much here. Your dad ever lose any business with any guys who felt that way?"

Jessie nodded. There had been a pair of guys who had felt that way and had relocated on another boat. "Yup. Some. But Dad says a whole lot more are into repeat business because of me. So, he figures he is ahead," she replied.

The rest of the table nodded their heads.

"You ever wonder about anyone coming on to you, if you were Captain?" Susie asked her privately. They had wandered off and were standing outside, watching people go by.

"I've got a mean gaff. I'll just carry it, if I need to. They should get the right idea from that," Jessie replied, shrugging her shoulders.

"Let's find each other again," Susie said. "I think we could be friends but I need to get home. Here's my phone number. Call sometime."

"Sure. Sleep tight," Jessie responded. She twiggled her fingers at Susie and went back to her truck and started home.

14

The next morning before any customers had arrived, Jessie asked her dad, "Could you validate the hours I have worked for you? I will need that validation if I decide to try for a Captain's license." She went on nervously, "I can get the record of my hours from my diary."

Bob stopped, a bit surprised as Jessie had never mentioned this to him before. He tented his fingers and tapped them on his nose as he looked at Jessie. "Sure," he said slowly. "If you complete the Coast Guard form, compose the letter and keep track of the hours, I will sign it."

He looked at Jessie closely. She seemed ok. "What brought this on, anyway?"

"I've kind of thought I would like to have that piece of paper, even if I never use it," Jessie responded.

Bob nodded. "This is not a woman's job but I can't think

of any reason you couldn't pass the test after you have your fifth season finished. You should have enough hours then." He paused again, "You are capable of being a good captain or doing anything you set your mind to."

Bob tapped his pipe on the railing to empty it and began to load it. He was pensive and Jessie did not interrupt his thoughts. He lit the pipe and shrugged his shoulders. He stopped and looked Jessie. "I like the idea of your trying for a Captain's license. Nothing ventured. Nothing gained. Who knows, it might work out just fine."

Jessie smiled. "Nothing like an unbiased opinion. You think I can do anything. You should have heard the boys last night when I asked about an '88. And then when I mentioned that I'd like to be a captain, they really exploded." They were both laughing when the first customers showed up.

The fishing that day was slow and a fog began to move in later in the day. It grew thicker and thicker and finally they could not see from one end to the other of the boat. Almost everyone had caught one or two salmon so Bob announced that they were going to leave for home early as it could take extra time to get home.

Jessie was astounded at how thick the fog was. She popped her head in and asked her dad, "How can you find the harbor in this?" and she waved her hand at the outside weather. Bob nodded. "You kind of have to kind of feel your way home. A bit like braille, to get there," he answered. "Basically, you go east, using your compass, and watching your depth finder to get to a 30 foot depth. Then, you go south keeping the boat at the 30 foot depth." Jessie nodded. She knew they had gone north of the harbor to find the fish. "How will you know when we are at the harbor?"

"You keep your eyes on the depth finder. When there is a drop or a deeper spot on your way south, you know you have found the channel to the harbor. It is a deep channel and you basically follow it due east to the harbor. Once you are anywhere near the harbor, the buoys will be up and you can hear them if there is any wind. You can hear the fog horn. You'll find your way in with no problems. Like I said. You feel your way, very much like braille, because you sure can't see anything." He paused. "You had probably better go back out and explain to our guests what is happening. Some of them might wonder how we can get through this pea soup."

15

In August, they changed fishing methods from predominately silver to king salmon. The kings were bigger and Captain Martin had Jessie keep the heads on the herring bait. The trolling was generally less deep but as the season went on, the salmon got larger and larger. Some were sixty pounds and more. It was not unusual when a "Fish on!" call to Jessie to come help a fisherman could get pretty confusing. The salmon would fight and swim up to the surface which caused the line to go over the lines of other fishermen on the boat. Getting tangled and untangled became part of a normal day.

Occasionally, some of the guests entered the "Salmon Derby" contest to see who caught the biggest fish that day. The contest was sponsored by the Westport Charter Boat Association. To enter cost a buck a ticket. The customers would enter in the morning before anyone was out to fish. The daily prize was good and the biggest catch of the season won $5000.00. So, hauling in a really big salmon got very exciting. The carnival atmosphere in Westport got higher and higher as the season wore on and the sixty plus pound plus fish were registered.

The king salmon were generally bigger than the silver but both species got heavier as the season progressed. At the end of the day, the fisherman who caught the biggest fish that day would go over to the Derby booth to get his fish weighed. There were up to a hundred people milling around the booth, which was on the harbor side of the street, to see the fish and wait so see who would bring in the biggest fish for the day.

It was a rowdy, cheerful crowd. Beer was plentiful and there was a lot of side betting.

Captain Martin and Jessie would go over to the booth if their fisherman had caught an exceptionally big salmon, to see how they measured up. The prize for the biggest fish for the day was large also. So the competition was heated every day.

Jessie and her dad would return to the boat once they found out the size of the winning salmon. They then went into their daily routine of cleaning the boat and getting ready for the next day's fishing.

Jessie liked the days when one of the fishermen would catch a really big salmon. Her tips were always larger and all of the customers left with big smiles on their faces.

"Jessie!" they would say. "You brought me luck.!"

16

In late August, on a windy and stormy day, the ocean was too rough and the salmon fishing for the day had been canceled. Jessie began to think about a car. There had been nothing that had interested her in the newspaper ads all summer. So, she decided she needed to visit the car dealerships in Aberdeen.

"Dad," she said. "I'd like to start looking for a car. May I take your car into Aberdeen to look?"

"Sure."

"You have any tips to give me?"

"Owning a car is a big job. You'll need to learn about the maintenance of a car, about insurance, about gas. You'll get to put your own gas in. Lots of fun. Lots of fun. You sure you want to get into all of this?" he asked, with a big grin on his face.

"Well, gee. Everyone and their dog have a car. It can't be all that hard," Jessie retorted.

Bob laughed. "Actually, learning some things about the maintenance of the motor are good to know. You have to do some of the same things with boat motors. If you do get to captain a ship, you'll need to know some of these things. You taking Susie with you?"

"Ah, gee. Of course. Her day has been cancelled too!"

Susie agreed enthusiastically. "I wondered what I was going to do with a day to myself. Only about eight gazillion things occurred to me, none of which sounded like fun. However, looking for a car for you sounds like fun, for sure. I can be a big help with finding a good color."

"What kind of car are you thinking about?" Susie asked on their way into Aberdeen.

"Mmmm. Something big. Dinky cars give me hay fever. Dad thinks I should look for an '88," Jessie laughed.

"Ohhhh. Great. Then I am going to vote for red. What is an '88?" Susie asked, laughing too.

"An '88 is a big Oldsmobile. Dad says it's a muscle car. Did you ever hear that before?"

They pulled into the first dealership. The rain was whipping around the buildings and there was no sign of a salesman.

Jessie looked around and laughed. "I guess we won't be high pressured by the sales staff as they apparently don't like this weather."

Just then, a heavyset man wrapped in a yellow raincoat, carrying an umbrella that kept getting blown inside out approached them. After a few times of turning the umbrella towards the wind to get it straight again, he gave up and folded it and set it on the ground.

He looked at them and grinned. "I guess you are desperate for a car to be shopping on a day like this. That's good because I will probably take any price for a car so that I can go back inside and stay dry. My name is Ben, by the way."

The whipping wind had blurred out some of his words, but the girls got the gist of what he was saying. They grinned.

"What can I help you find?" he asked.

"I need a good used car, preferably an '88," Jessie responded. "If you can show me where they are, I can look on my own and then come find you when I need more information."

"You can do that if you want. The year and price are marked on each of the front windows. However, I don't think we have a used '88 in stock. But if you want to look through the cars we do have, we can go for a test drive if you find one you like.

The wind was whipping their rain coats and the rain was still falling in sheets. Ben looked at the girls and said, "It is almost impossible to hear you talk, so I am thinking I will wait for you inside. If you find one that you like, holler."

So, Jessie and Susie wandered through the used cars on their own.

"What do you think, Jessie? I haven't seen a single bright red one."

"I think I should come back later if I can't find an '88. I'd like to see one first before I try any other car. Ben may not get a sale from us today." Jessie had to shout so that Susie could hear her.

"And this isn't the most wonderful weather for being outside. Old Ben probably has the right idea."

Susie nodded.

The girls made their way back to the dealership office and found the big man. He met them at the door. "Find something you would like to test drive?" he asked.

"I'm going to try to find an '88 and if can't find one I like, I'll shop for one of the other cars." Jessie responded.

When they were back in Susie's car, she laughed and laughed. "Boy, he was some salesman."

They drove to the next car lot and the weather eased up a bit. At least you could hear people talk. The salesman, named George, had an '88 and was ready for Jessie to test drive it. It was a light green and about five years old and Jessie liked the looks of it.

"I would like to test drive it," Jessie told the salesman.

" O.K. I'll go get the keys," he said.

"You coming along for the drive?" Jessie asked Susie.

"I don't know. It isn't bright red. I'll have to give it some thought," Susie said with a very straight fact, trying not to laugh.

Jessie gave her a dirty look. Susie did laugh then.

The test drive felt good to Jessie. "I'll have my Dad look at this and then I will make up my mind," she told the salesman.

On the way home, Jessie commented, "I sure hope if I have to look at any more cars that the weather will be nicer."

The storm was slowing a bit but was still causing the harbor water to chop wildly. The girls could catch glimpses through the rain. "Not a good day to be on the water," Susie said.

That evening, the pot roast was good and hot and everyone was enjoying the meal. Jessie had recounted the car buying expedition, which was causing a lot of laughter.

"Dealing with used car salesmen isn't fun," Betty commented.

Bob laughed. "I'll try to get to Aberdeen tomorrow after work, to check out that car," he said.

"I'll take care of cleaning the cabin and locking up to save you some time. If you want to get an earlier start," Jessie responded with a smile.

Bob nodded. "Sure thing."

17

The storm had passed and the day was sunny and bright.

"You guys go out in that storm yesterday?" one of the guests asked.

"Never," Captain Martin responded, "That strong of a storm can cause major problems for this size of boat." He paused a moment.

"It can cause problems for bigger boats too, for that matter," he continued. "No one goes to sea voluntarily in that kind of weather and if you are caught in it while at sea, you just have to hunker down."

The storm had roiled the ocean and the fishing was very good that day. All of the fishermen had caught their limit ... limited ... by noon. After getting everyone back to the dock and the boat ready for the next day, there was plenty of daylight for Bob to go to Aberdeen.

He looked over the cars Jessie had liked and selected the newer one to take to the mechanic. Jimson inspected the car very carefully. "The brakes need to be replaced and the transmission is getting some worn spots," he reported. "But I have an idea for you. You remember Buck Sprints? He worked for me up until a couple of years ago," he asked Bob.

"Sure. He was a good mechanic. What happened to him?" Bob asked.

"He decided to go back to school and finish his degree so he could teach. Wanted a steadier paycheck than mechanic pay. But the reason I mentioned him is, he has an '88 he needs to sell. He needs a newer car. Maybe you could look at his old car. It is undoubtedly in good shape."

Bob nodded his head. "Sounds like a good idea. You have his phone number?"

Bob returned the car to the dealership, telling them he needed to think about it some more. The phone call to Buck resulted in Bob and Jessie going over to his house the next day. The car was in a garage and was spotless, waxed and declared to be in good shape.

"You need a good price for this?" Bob asked him.

Jessie looked at the '88 and got into the driver's seat. She liked the feel of it. "O.K. if we take it for a bit of a drive?" she asked Buck.

"Sure," he responded, "Let me go get the keys for you."

Jessie loved it. She loved the bigness of the car. The smooth drive soothed her. It had a heavy careful feeling but would leap when she pushed the gas petal. Bob was smiling and nodding his head.

"What do you think?" Buck asked when they returned.

Bob was nodding his head. "If the price is right, we surely like the vehicle," he said.

"Two hundred dollars."

"Sold."

Jessie started driving herself to work after she had her car. Her dad showed her how to gas it, how to check the oil, how to add oil or change it. How and when to get new spark plugs. He told her what air pressure was best for the tires and showed her how to check the pressure. He showed her the spare tire and had her change a tire, to make sure she could. He told her what to listen for to make sure timing was right.

"A lot of things about maintaining the motor and mechanics of a car are also useful to know for the running of a boat. This is generally good information for you to have," he told Jessie.

"I hope I don't have to change a tire when out to sea. I can just barely do it on solid ground," she responded.

18

"Kevin. Thanks for the job. I like being on the ocean every day."

Kevin was about her dad's age but heavier. He was barrel chested and was prematurely bald with just a fringe of dark hair around his ears. He usually wore a hat and dark glasses and was almost always grinning. He laughed a lot. He owned his boat and only fished on weekends until school was out and then it was seven days a week like the rest of the fleet. He taught the U.S. history class at Aberdeen High School along with algebra and geometry.

"You'll earn your way and I have a good deckhand," he replied. "And you talk so much on board ... keeps me from having to talk so much," he added. Jessie was notoriously quiet on shore but loved talking with the customers."

"There are a few things I do differently from your dad. It you have any questions, just ask."

"They were sitting in the galley, Kevin was drinking a cup of coffee, Jessie had her tea. He was one of Jessie's favorite people. He was used to kids her age and she was comfortable with him."

"There is one thing and it has nothing to do with the way you run your boat," she said to him.

Kevin raised his eyebrows, but said nothing."

"I've been thinking," she continued, "about getting a Captain's License." She stopped and looked at him to see what his reaction to this statement was. Kevin didn't blink an eye.

"So, she continued on, "It may not do me a bit of good. But I guess I think it would be nice to have that piece of paper. It might be kind of foolish but I was wondering if you would certify my hours. Dad certified the hours I worked for him. He had me keep track and then I wrote the letter giving the information and he signed it. No muss, no fuss type of thing."

He still said nothing.

"I keep a diary and can give you the total hours at the end of this season and next, if I'm still working for you."

Kevin seemed deep in thought. He finally nodded his head.

"There's nothing wrong with your getting a license. I do think you could eventually captain a boat for someone." He was pensive and spoke slowly, "This has been a man's job forever in Westport. But that's no reason you might not be hired. I will sure teach you everything I can."

He was still nodding, as much to himself as to Jessie.

"The big catch for you is being a captain and being good at it. Not just as a fad or a novelty," he paused again. "But for crying in the bucket, Jessie. Would you try to grow a bit? Things would go a lot easier if you weren't so darned dinky," and he laughed at his own joke.

The next morning, she was a little early. It felt a little odd to not be deckhanding for her father, but Jessie got the ice and herring and was ready for the day. The **Water Dancer** had had a complete paint job along with its normal annual maintenance over the winter and she looked really good.

Captain Kevin showed up at his normal time.

"Hello, Jessie," he called out from the float.

"Hello, Captain Sir. Welcome aboard. You want to be whistled on or something?"

"Oh. Lordy, no. Had enough of the Navy when I was there," he laughed.

The weather was clear and the sun had risen enough to cast long shadows. The seagulls were flopping around looking for something to eat.

"This is kind of a postcard day for fishing," Captain Kevin said as he stepped onto the deck.

"Yup, Captain Sir," Jessie said with a curt salute.

"Be careful with the salute, Jessie," he said, "or you will get an eyeful of fish guck on your face."

Jessie looked at her hands. She was working bare handed and the herring slime and some scales were on her hands. "Yup," she thought to herself, "I could get an eyeful."

She finished the bait and got the sinkers on the poles, ready for the guests. It was going to be a glorious day. The air was dense, cool and moist. She could smell the seaweed in it. It smelled great to Jessie. The silly birds were squawk-ing and there was a harbor seal poking around the float.

"I wonder where the rest of his family is," Jessy thought to herself. His sleek glossy head shown with the sunshine on it. What a wonderful way to earn a living, being on the ocean.

The first of the fishermen began to arrive and getting them signed on and showing them where to stow their rain gear and lunches kept her busy for a while. Then, finally, the last two arrived talking and laughing. They stepped onto the deck and spotted Jessie. They had fished with her dad that previous year and remembered her.

"Hey, Jessie," one of them called out. "Where is the fight chair?" This was an old joke and Jessie had heard it before. A fight chair is used for big game fish when there was only one person fishing on a boat. The chair has straps to hold the fisherman in the chair while he is landing a big fish. Fight chairs were definitely not used on the charter salmon boats in Westport.

"Well, guys. Just follow me," and she motioned for them to follow her. She led them straight to the toilet and said, "If you need straps to keep your seat, please let us know."

This always got a good laugh from everyone within earshot.

Jessie was wearing her hair in a single braid that day with the braid coming out of the back of a ball cap. She had on dark glasses and wore dark green waterproof bib overalls with a light sweater under a heavier sweater. Her rain gear, which she kept stashed in the cabin for the days she would need it, included a hooded slicker and a sou'wester style hat. She kept toenail clippers in her pocket to cut fishing lines if they got really tangled. When she was first deckhanding, she kept the clippers on a lanyard around her neck until she caught it on something and got a good choking out of it. She never wore anything around her neck after that. Certainly, no necklace or hooded sweatshirts with strings. Nothing. These things could get caught up and become very dangerous.

After her normal morning routine and the bait preparation was finished, she wore a glove with no fingers on them. Sometimes she wore a fingerless glove on just one hand. The protected her hands against sharp fish teeth, gills, spines or hooks. The glove was a rubber backed fabric. If the weather was cold, she would wear both gloves. After her first summer of wearing tennies, she had found a pair of brown heavy leather boots. Altogether, her outfit was well suited for her work.

Kevin was scouting for salmon when he caught sight of dark birds fluttering and diving into the water from time to time. They were probably feeding and they liked the same type of food that salmon liked. So Kevin headed straight for the birds and found what looked like salmon on his fish-finder.

"Get everyone baited and ready to fish. It looks like 30 feet of line should work."

Soon people began to get bites and some yelled, "Fish On." So, Jessie would grab a salmon net to help them land their fish.

After a bit, when there was a lull, Jessie asked Kevin why these birds were called "whale birds."

"They are Sooty Shearwaters. But they are called "whale birds" because they used to help the whalers, a long time ago, find whales. But then I heard from another guy that they used to following the whaling ships that threw garbage and stuff overboard. A lot of that stuff made a good meal for them."

He paused, "I don't know which story is correct." Just then a guest called out, "Fish on!!" and Jessie was again busy helping the guests.

19

During her fifth summer, she found a roommate and an apartment. Sandy's father owned a charter company and the two girls had decided to strike out on their own when Sandy had found out that an apartment above the ice cream shop was available. Sandy worked seven days a week for her dad and had very similar hours to Jessie.

"One of us can cook and the other clean up when we decide to eat in," Sandy said. "And we can trade off the cooking every other time and split the cost of groceries," Jessie added. Their routine was simple and worked for them. Sandy chatted and Jessie nodded. They got along well.

"Jessie," Sandy asked one night when she was finishing the dishes and cleaning up after supper. "Are you still thinking about taking the test to get a captain's license?"

"I'm keeping track of the days I've worked. I could have enough by the end of this season. Are you thinking about taking the test?"

"No. No. No. Noooooooooooooo," Sandy laughed. "I cannot imagine having to deal with all these fishermen or even these smart aleck deckhands, much less run a boat with all the responsibilities that entails." She stopped and looked at Jessie. "You going to own your own boat?"

"Nope. Can't even begin to afford one."

Jessie smiled at Sandy. "I know what you're thinking but truthfully, I am not even sure there are any boat owners who would hire a woman to captain their boat, so I might not ever be employed.

She was frowning with her head down as she thought about it. "I might find some second captain work."

Sandy nodded. Second captain work was for fishing trips that lasted more than one day. The boat had to have a second captain so the first one could get some sleep.

Jessie continued. "I just kind of like the idea of having that piece of paper that says I am eligible to captain a boat. The other deckhands all think I'm wasting my time. But Dad and Kevin both undertook to train me and help me figure out the ins and outs of captaining. Captain Kevin has had some girls do pretty well in his classes. I guess he thinks I can do the same thing with the Captain's test."

"Well," Sandy responded, "If you get your license and end up running a boat for someone, I'll bet there will be several Westport women who will get their licenses also. They would do it now, but they are thinking they would be laughed at."

Jessie laughed at that. "Well, being laughed at by the likes of Jim Bob won't bother me much." Sandy laughed at that. Jim Bob was one of the deckhands on another boat who was always cheerful and flirted with the girls shamelessly.

Jessie continued, "Captain Kevin is showing me the mechanics of the boat. He has shown me how to use the fish-finder. Tricks for steering. Being aware of the wind ... the currents ... the weather reports ... how to use the radios. He thinks a woman could make a very good captain if they were given the chance. So, I will see if I can pass the test and get a license. It's kind of like buying a ticket for the lottery. If you don't buy a ticket, you have no chance to win. I would never know if it could work out."

"Well, that is true enough. I am sure rooting for you," Sandy replied.

By the end of that season, Jessie had two certified letters. One signed by her dad and the other signed by Captain Kevin. They verified she had served enough time on the boats to be eligible to take the Master's test.

20

The drive to Seattle seemed to take forever. It was dark, mid March, and early in the morning. The trip was actually about two hours, but seemed like four. Jessie was a little anxious about the test. She had very little idea about what information was needed for the test and she had not prepared for it at all, except for paying close attention and asking questions for the past five years.

How hard could it be? All kinds of people had passed it before. Well, she would soon know but time was sure dragging.

Finally, the lights of Seattle appeared and she found her way to the Coast Guard building. The lawns and sidewalks were neat and the entrance smelled of wax from the floors. She asked the young man at the information window where the Captain's licensing test was being given. He nodded at her and picked up a phone and made a brief comment that Jessie did not catch.

"If you would wait, Chief Sanders will be here in a sec to take you to the room," the young man offered.

Chief Sanders appeared and asked to see some identification which he checked against a typed list he was holding and very soon she was being shown to the testing room.

The room had high school type desks, a chalk board at the front of the room and looked very ordinary. There were already two men sitting at a couple of the desks.

"Are you administering the test?" she asked Chief Sanders.

"Yes. I give the tests and do the timing," he answered.

"How many of us do you expect?"

He was smiling. "We are looking for five today.

He left the room and Jessie settled herself into a desk and looked out the windows. The morning light was hazy and the trees were bare. Typical, thought Jessie to herself.

Chief Sanders returned with two more men who settled themselves into desks also.

The chief began "This test is in four sections. There will be 90 minutes for each section. You will take two sections this morning and then two this afternoon. There will be a short, fifteen minutes, coffee break in the middle of each section and the lunch hour will be from twelve to one. The restrooms are out the door and to your right. I'll give you a five minute warning that the time for each test is almost up."

He paused and the group all nodded. Then he continued, "You must pass all four sections. However, if you fail one or more sections, you may take them again. The materials on the front table are navigational charts, tide tables and other information that you may use. Do you have any questions?"

No response.

So, he handed each person the test and sat down at the front table and set his timer and said, "Good luck to you all. You may begin."

Jessie filled in her name, address, social security number and date of birth. She looked at the first question and slowly began to fill in answers. Time passed. The second section seemed more complicated and there were many questions she just did not know, but she kept on.

Jessie ate a cheese sandwich and had a cup of tea for lunch. The other men talked a little to each other but said nothing to Jessie.

When the last section was over, Chief Sanders told her she had passed one section but not the other three. He asked her if she wanted to return to try the other three sections again.

"I do want to try again," she said.

Sanders was very polite and smiled. "Don't worry. Most of the guys who take this test don't pass all four sections the first time they try."

Jessie nodded and left, still in a daze.

"I can't believe how much I didn't know," she thought to herself when she left the building.

Jessie was very tired from spending the whole day taking the test. She was discouraged. "This is ridiculous," she said to herself. "I can pass that test. The next test time is in another month. I need to apply myself. I can do this," she repeated. "I wonder if Mom would mind if I stayed in my old room in Seattle while I work on getting this information absorbed."

Jessie's mom was delighted to have her.

"Sweetie. That first test was a practice test. Now you know what you need to do, you can do it."

Getting ready for the test required a lot of memorization for facts and information she would use only for the test.

Some of the memorized stuff was things like the navigational lights for different kinds of boats like fishing boats, tugboats, ships, sail boats and seaplanes. Each type of ship had its own style of lights suspended from their antennae or towers.

She learned that different areas had buoys with singular colors, horn, bell and timed blinking lights. So, Jessie spent the next four weeks buried in navigational charts, how to chart courses from Westport to Astoria, Raymond to Whidby Island. She memorized the Coast Guard flags and their meanings.

She made herself flashcards for a lot of the terminology. She grilled herself over and over. She practiced plotting courses with a chart, a slide rule and a compass.

She knew what to expect the next time she showed up for the test.

23

Chief Sanders was there again. He smiled when he saw Jessie come in. "I'm glad you're trying again," he said. "Some of these guys get discouraged and don't come back."

She sat at the table and eventually started the first section handed to her. The questions made better sense this time and by the end of the day, she felt hopeful when she handed Sanders her last section

Chief Sanders had been grading her work and told her to please wait a few minutes while he finished grading her last section. Jessie waited. It was hard to breathe. She really needed to get out of there, but she sat and waited.

He finally looked up. It had been fifteen minutes, but it felt like hours. He smiled.

"Congratulations. You have passed all four sections. You may skipper a charter boat up to twenty miles out on the ocean from Willapa to Cape Elizabeth. That sound good?" he asked with a big grin on his face.

Jessie couldn't speak. She just gave a weak smile and nodded. She got up and left the room. When she passed the first door in the hallway, it opened and a young man looked out. He spotted her. "Congratulations," he called out to her.

The next door opened and a head looked out. "Good for you," called out a young woman. A man came up behind the woman and nodded at Jessie.

Jessie was bemused. It was like whack a mole. The doors opened and heads popped out. The word had got out in the building that a young woman, not yet twenty- one had passed the test. Everyone was amazed. There had never been a woman pass the test and no one under twenty-one had ever passed it either. She left the building, still in a daze. But this time she was bursting to tell someone she had made it.

SHE HAD MADE IT.

She went back to her Mom's house. Her mother was at a meeting that day and had not returned. Jessie went to the phone. Her dad was out of reach also. Who to call? She dialed Kevin's number and he answered.

"Kevin. It's Jessie. I passed. I passed!"

"Jessie. That is terrific! You just finished the test? Let me tell honey bunch here." She could hear him calling out to his wife to share the news. He came back to the phone laughing. "We've agreed that you really should have wait-ed until you were twenty-one, so we could go out and really celebrate."

Jessie was laughing too. "Well, have a beer on me," she replied.

"Beer, heck," he returned. "It's got to be champagne." He paused for a second and then said in serious tones. "I suppose you're going to be too good to just be a deckhand any more so I will have to find someone to replace you."

"I doubt if anyone will hire me as a captain so I'd better not be too good to deckhand," she replied gleefully. "But I've got this piece of paper and I'm tickled pink to have it."

Kevin laughed, "Your time will come. Looking like a fourteen year old is going to be interesting. I sure wish I could be on deck when you do first captain a boat."

Jessie smiled to herself. Chances were that she would probably never captain a boat. However, she was pleased to hear Kevin talk about her having her own boat.

Her mom returned about a half hour later.

"My heavens," she exclaimed when she heard the news. "When your stepdad gets home, we need to all go out for supper and celebrate."

Jessie began to feel like a balloon that had had all of the air let out of it. She nodded to her mom.

"That would be great."

Jessie was sitting on the couch with all of the energy of a rag doll but she was still smiling. She looked at her mom and said, "Kevin thinks I should have waited until I was twenty-one to pass the test so we could "really" go out and celebrate.

Her mom laughed. "And have a terrific hangover to-morrow. But he's got a point. He's got a point."

23

Jessie started deckhanding for Kevin as soon as the season opened. The routine was familiar and she was glad to be back at work.

"Kevin. You know, most of those questions on that test are so far out of the ordinary. I'll never use that stuff."

Kevin nodded. "I think they do that to winnow out half baked applicants. But I thought the same thing when I took the test."

He paused. "You know, Jessie. If you don't get a boat right away, you could second captain for the tuna boats."

Jessie nodded.

"I thought of that too. To second captain for a boat, you are essentially only responsible for the boat. All of the fishing decisions are up to the captain? Right?"

Kevin nodded again.

"If they can stay within my license limit, it might work," she responded as much to herself as to Kevin.

When the first customers came on, they seemed a bit odd. They kept looking at her and murmuring between themselves. Jessie shrugged and smilingly made sure they had signed the sign-up sheet to get their number for the day and to make sure they knew where to stow their lunches and gear.

When the last customer finally arrived, she understood all of the furtiveness. He brought a big sheet cake that said, "Congratulations Lady Captain" on it.

Everyone hooted and hollered and made a great deal of noise. The customers on the boats in nearby slips asked what was going on and their captains told them and they joined the hoorahing too. The word spread quickly and most of float 8 was whooping. All in all, it was a pretty funny experience and Jessie and her customers were all tickled.

"We can get into that cake in a bit," Kevin called out. "We need to get going so we don't miss any fishing time."

Jessie was pleased. She started baiting the poles and getting ready for the day. It was a fairly normal day except for the cake, coffee and party in the middle of it.

That night, she radioed her dad because he was in California. She called him on a single side band long range radio and told him about the event. He laughed and laughed. "That's pretty funny about the other boats joining in," he said. "Was the fishing good today"

Captain Martin kept track of the salmon fishing and how it was faring. Even tho he was busy with his tugboat work, he still watched carefully. He was right in that fewer people signed on to fish for salmon. The industry, as a whole, was making less money.

24

In early July, Jessie was over at her dad's having supper. She was going to babysit for her parents for the evening and had been invited for supper. While she was helping Betty by setting the table, the phone rang. Betty answered it and looked at Jenny.

"It's for you."

"Jenny," the voice said. "This is Neddie Rose. Is this a good time to talk?"

"Sure. What can I do for you," Jessie asked.

"I know it almost supper time, so I'll be quick. I need to know if you would be willing to captain the **Blue Water** for me? You'll need to look at her and see if she would do. She's docked at float three," she paused.

Jessie found she was holding her breath and couldn't talk. The surprise was total.

So Neddie Rose continued. "If you do like her, we can work out the details later but I think you and your new license will fit in nicely with my company."

Jessie choked but managed to kind of croak, "I'd be delighted."

Neddie Rose gave a laugh. "Good. Call me after you have inspected her and decided. I'll let you get back to your supper" and she hung up.

Jessie was all amazement. She was breathing again but speechless. "She must think I am an idiot," she said out loud.

Betty looked at her with a questioning look on her face. That remark had not made a bit of sense. Captain Martin came into the dining room just then. He looked from wife to daughter and wondered what was going on.

"Hey, Dad," she called as she returned to the dining room. "You won't believe. You won't believe."

He looked at her. Betty was shrugging her shoulders. Jessie was usually quiet but when she did talk, she was usually articulate. She seemed to be having problems speaking at this time. Betty came in carrying a bowl of mashed potatoes and a bowl of peas to go with the Swedish meatballs and gravy. She looked at her stepdaughter and laughed. Jessie was the picture of excitement.

"What's up, Jessie?" she asked.

"Neddie Rose just called and she has a boat she wants me to run," Jessie almost screeched. She began to bounce up and down.

Bob said nothing for a minute and then burst out laughing. "Good for you!"

"Which boat," he asked.

"The **Blue Water**. It's on float three. Do you know her?" she asked.

Bob thought for a moment. "I don't think so."

"She wants me to look at her tomorrow to see if she would be o.k."

"If she is not actively sinking, I'd bet that she would work out," Bob replied. "Let's go look at her tomorrow after work. Deal?" he asked.

"Deal," Jessie answered.

"I'd like to eat now while the food is hot," he added.

Jessie looked at the table. Swedish meatballs was one of her favorite suppers and she was hungry. Indecision immobilized her again.

Bob and Betty looked at her again and laughed and they began to eat. Sammy was using a fork and knife now but could not capture the meatballs to cut them into smaller pieces. Betty was helping him.

Sammy looked up. "Gessie going to be a Captain too?"

"Yup." Jessie looked at him and tousled his hair. Captain Martin the Second," she pronounced.

"Captain Martin Jr.?" offered Betty.

It was hard to get to sleep that night. She had rehashed the telephone conversation over with Sandy and the enormity of the event finally sank in. "I've been feeling like I'm twelve again," Jessie told Sandy. "No control over my life at all. I'm having problems trying to feel calm and adult like over all of this."

Sandy laughed. "Well, yesssssssssssss. I can see your point. Geeee whizzzzzzzzzzzz, you're twenty-one now."

25

After work that next day, Bob, Kevin and Jessie went over to float three. Bob and Kevin were intensely interested in the boat. They inspected it from head to toe. The paint job was new, but the boat was older. But, by and large, it looked like it would float just fine. Bob had stopped by Neddie Rose's office and picked up a key. So, they started the boat, listened to the engines and took her out to the harbor. Both men decided there needed to be more ballast and it needed to be better placed.

Jessie wanted to clean up the cabin area and get the tools and equipment better sorted. She and her dad spent two days after work getting the **Blue Waters** ready. Jessie signed the contract to run the boat and Neddie Rose asked her to be ready for customers by that next Friday.

"If you're needing a good deckhand," Bob told her, "I saw Donny Braxton yesterday and he said he was looking for a job. He had applied for your job with Kevin, but Kevin had already found a replacement. Donny worked for me for a couple of summers and was good and reliable. He said he would have dinner at the A1. Shall we go see if he is there yet?"

"That sounds good to me. I remember him."

They walked over to the restaurant talking about the **Blue Waters** and what it would be like to captain for Neddie Rose. The A1 was shaped like a big ell, so almost all of the tables were in view from the entrance. Jessie fluttered her fingers at her Dad and pointed to the kitchen area with a questioning look on her face. Bob nodded and went directly to Donny's table. "Jessie will be here in a minute. She's saying hi to the cook."

Donny grinned. "And owner," he finished for Bob.

A hurried waitress paused by the table. "You want a menu?" she asked.

"No thanks. Just bring a cup of coffee for me and tea for Jessie."

"She should be through bugging the cook soon."

The waitress gave a short laugh and left.

Jessie poked her face into the kitchen area and saw Hilary was waiting tables that evening and Rod was cooking. They both looked up and smiled and nodded at her.

"Guess what," Jessie said to them.

They were both busy but they looked at her and shrugged.

"I have a boat to captain. I'll be working for Neddie Rose."

They both stopped then and gave her a big smile.

"Hooray!" Hilary said. "All right!" Rob added. "We'll be sure and tell Harry when he comes in."

Jessie backed out and went to Donny's table. He looked at her and said, "Your dad has been filling me in on the big news."

Jessie smiled. "Any chance you could deckhand for me starting Friday?"

Donny was red haired and a practical joker. He was freckled and always had a smile on his face. He had been gone from Westport for a couple of years as his wife had been ill and needed to be closer to a big hospital. "I think being a deckhand for you would be one of the more interesting experiences of my life. It would be a pleasure."

26

Friday morning, she filled two big thermos jugs with coffee and had hot water in a third one. She had her usual three cheese sandwiches and three Three Musketeers candy bars ready to go. When she had everything ready, she hauled them out to her '88 and climbed in.

At the office, she took a deep breath. This was going to be quite a day. Her biggest worry was docking the **Blue Waters**. She had only docked it once and did not have the technique quite right. Getting the speed slow enough to dock well was different for each boat and took a few times to learn what worked for each boat. Nothing else was of any problem today except for the docking. If she came in too fast there would be a heavy thump and jolt when it hit the dock. Might even upend a customer so it paid to be careful. However, coming in way slow was embarrassing, so Jessie's main worry was docking. The rest of the day should be routine.

Neddie Rose was at the desk and she was smiling broadly at Jessie. "Good morning, Captain Martin," she said.

"Captain Martin is my dad. I don't think this is going to work," Jessie responded. She had stopped dead in her tracks when the thought hit her.

"Mmmmm. Captain Jessie then?" Neddie Rose responded.

"We are putting all of the Captain's full names on our roster, just so we can be clear about you. Oh. And I'll need a picture of you."

Jessie nodded. "You have my list for today?"

Neddie Rose nodded also and handed Jessie the list of customers slated to go on her boat that day. "I have fifteen boats out today, including yours. Our CB channel is 15. I know you know Carl, so you can ask him about finding fish if you're having problems locating them, or about where you found the fish so everyone can share the info. Oh, speak of the devil, here's Carl now."

Jessie turned around and smiled at Carl. He beamed at her. "Wow. Our first lady captain. Are we modern or what?"

He strode over to Jessie and shook her hand. "You are welcome to follow me out. We usually find the fish ... there are quite a few of us and that helps."

"Thanks," Jessie responded. A couple more of the captains came into the office and they also congratulated Jessie. She told them all thanks and turned to Neddie Rose. "Thanks for this," she said and made for a great escape. All of this attention was a little overwhelming and she was getting embarrassed. She just hoped Donny would be at the boat getting ready. She was really really not used to this amount of attention. Getting onto the boat was going to be a big relief.

She headed out and down float three. There was the bright yellow **Blue Waters** waiting and Donny was busy with the bait. She laughed to herself. Who would have thought that getting to this boat on her first day was going to be such a relief?

Donny spotted her and waved.

"Hi, Donny," she said as she hopped on board.

"Hi, Captain Mar..." and he stopped with a confused look on his face.

"Captain Jessie sounds good to me. Would that work for you?" she asked the befuddled Donny.

He nodded and was laughing at himself. "Captain Jessie is great. Saying Captain Martin would probably paralyze me if I was trying to use it."

Jessie laughed.

She stowed her lunch and gear and then started the engine. She had been running it the previous evening to make sure it was ok and had filled the diesel and water tanks in preparation for her first day. It started and sounded good.

Donny stuck his head into the cabin. "Everything OK in here?" he asked. "Everything shipshape?"

"I'm not worried about getting out or even finding fish," Jessie replied. "I only hope I can dock the **Blue Waters** without banging the boat too hard."

"If you come in too slow, I'll get out and push," Donny volunteered. "Will that help?"

The customers began arriving. They knew they were sailing with a lady captain, but still the amazement on their faces when they shook hands with her was pronounced. No one expected a girl who looked like she was 14 to be taking them out that day. Donny laughed and told stories galore for several months about that first day.

27

A few days after her first day as captain, Donny greeted her waving a page from a newspaper. Jessie eyed him and shook her head.

"What now?" she asked him.

"You're in the Seattle paper."

Jessie shrugged her shoulders and said, "Oh, really. Well, gee whiz." And went into the cabin and started her normal routine for getting ready for the day fishing.

Donny laughed and followed her into the cabin. "I'll read it to you. OK. Here goes."

Jessica Martin First Licensed Woman Skipper, Says Coast Guard.

Shortly after she turned 21 last month, Jessica Martin was licensed by the U.S. Coast Guard to captain "mechanically propelled passenger vehicles under 50 tons."

Jessica, a diminutive 95-pounder standing 5-1, is the daughter of Marilyn Brown, former Port Townsend mayor now living in Seattle. She graduated from the local high school.

She subsequently spent most of her time as a deckhand for various charter companies in Westport. Her father, Robert Martin, currently operates a tugboat out of Hoquiam.

Jessica will skipper, as her first command, Westport's Islander Motel charter boat, "The Blue Waters." The boat carries a maximum of 12 passengers.

According to the Coast Guard, she is the first woman on the West Coast to obtain such a license – and also is probably the youngest of all skippers.

Commented the PI's Emmett Watson: "They've come a long way, baby, since it was bad luck to even have a woman aboard ship."

"Whaddya think?" he asked?

"Let me think. How does "Good Grief" sound?" Jessie responded. "That article has a few errors in it, like my being the only lady captain."

"Actually," she thought to herself, "it sounds like my mother wrote it."

Donny laughed. "That bad luck thing a pretty big issue here?"

Jessica shrugged. "You know. I've heard of it being a big deal on the East Coast, but it has never been much of an issue here in Westport or on the West Coast for all I know.

It probably got started on the big commercial fishing boats." She thought a moment. "Come to think of it, I can see where having a woman on board could cause friction. I can see where the notion would first start .... A hundred years ago."

"However," she continued, "charter fishing is more like Disneyland. Just here for entertainment, you know," she replied.

She started the engine and all sounded good.

28

Jessie's customers for the day arrived and soon they were on their way out to the open ocean. The fishing the day before had been slow, so Jessie was watching for sooty shearwaters. These were the black waterbirds that flocked to where the herring and other small fish were. These were the same fish salmon liked so the birds were a good sign that a school of salmon could be feeding in the area also. Jessie spotted a cluster of the birds on the water. Her customers put their lines out and she slowly trolled over the area where she had seen the birds. A passenger suddenly called out, "Fish on," and the day was started. She radioed the other Captains where she was and that the fish were biting. They spent most of their day in the area and everyone caught their limit of salmon. It was a good day of fishing.

Her second year of captaining was a little calmer for Jessie. Donny was still working for her. He never got tired of the double take from first time passengers when they found

Jessie was their captain for the day. But a whole lot of her customers were coming back for the second year, so apparently she was doing something right.

In August, on a lightly foggy day, they had left the harbor heading for the area that had had good fishing the day before. They were out on the open ocean and Jessie was watching the fish finder. Things seemed quite normal when a woman screamed. "I saw his feet. I saw his feet go by!"

Donny was there in a flash and then hollered, "Man overboard. Man overboard." He grabbed an orange life ring and ran to the back of the boat and heaved it in the man's direction. The man began swimming and was able to reach it. Jessie immediately cut the throttle and went out to see what happened.

Donny was pointing back and you could see, about a couple of hundred yards back, a man bobbing in the water. He was trying to wave at the boat. Jessie looked at Donny and said, "Get some of the customers to point their fingers at him. Don't take your eyes off of him and keep pointing. You got that?"

"Yup," Donny responded. He was staring at the bobbing head and pointing. "You can help by doing the same thing as Donny and get some coffee for him when we get him back on deck," she said to the woman who had seen his feet go over.

She went back and began to turn the boat back. She watched as Donny pivoted to keep his finger pointing at the man. It seemed like it took a very long time to get turned back. But the passengers were pointing. She aimed back at the general direction they were pointing and eventually she could see the man bobbing in the water. She slowed down and came along side of him.

Donny had a line with a weight attached. He threw it at the man as they neared. Jessie could see he was a younger man and he was trying to catch the line. When he caught hold of it, the motion of the boat pulled him along. "Hang on," Donny called out. The man was obviously getting tired but he clung to the line. The boat was near standstill and they put a light ladder that hung down the side of the boat and Donny got down the ladder and helped the man on it. The young man was near exhaustion and needed help to get up the ladder and onto the deck.

One very wet young man lay on the deck gasping and exhausted.

They assisted him into the cabin and got his soaked clothes off and replaced them with some dry ones from Donny.

Jessie brought him a couple of blankets and a lady passenger handed him a cup of hot coffee. He pulled himself up and leaned against the wall, still sitting on the floor. He sipped the coffee.

"This coffee tastes good," and his voice croaked. "Hard to talk," he added. Donny and another passenger hoisted the kid to his feet and took him outside to the deck. Shortly, they had him walking on his own.

Donny reported back to Jessie. "His name is Lou Hillman. He seems to be ok but he's pretty wobbly."

Lou broke in, "Thank you, Captain Jessie. That was scary." He was pale and obviously still a little confused.

"We'll take you right back to Westport. We can have an ambulance waiting if we think you're going to need it," Jessie responded.

She smiled at him and then looked at the other passengers. "We're going to return to Westport and will plan on fishing later than usual so you can all get a full day of fishing."

Jessie looked at Donny, "That was quick thinking to throw out the life ring for him." He smiled, "Basic training, mostly basic training."

That night, Jessie was on the phone telling her father about the day's misadventure. "I think he was possibly a little drunk but he said he was sea sick and was leaning over the railing and went too far," she told her dad.

"Mmmmm," Captain Martin said. "You do know that he, and you for that matter, are really lucky. He could have panicked or gone into shock with the cold water. It sounds like he was doing a pretty good job at staying calm enough to manage until you could get turned around."

Later in the season, Jessie and Donny had had good luck with the early fishing but it was getting foggier and foggier as the afternoon went by. "Poles up," Jessie said to Donny. "We're going to head back to port now. This fog is getting kind of bad. Donny was hollering "Poles up," to the customers when they came into a fog so thick it seems like a cotton ball. The guests got their poles up and Jessie turned the boat eastward. She remembered her dad's description on how to return to port with no visibility, but it still seemed a bit scary. She could not travel too fast as there would be no way to avoid another boat if she was going her normal speed. She headed toward the shore and after about an hour the depth finder registered 30 feet and she then steered the boat northward and kept watching the depth finder to stay at 30 feet and had the compass heading north. Another hour passed and the fog was still very thick. Finally, she saw the depth finder show a drop to 40 feet and was still dropping. Jessie turned the boat due east again and slowly came toward the harbor. She could hear the fog horns from the harbor area .

"Good," she thought to herself.

Somewhere there should be a way to the harbor's mouth. She watched the depth finder over the deeper water and then spotted a buoy. She knew where she was now and went on into Grays Harbor and over to the Westport marina with no problems.

Donny stuck his head in. "Good work, Captain Ma'am."

"Thanks," she answered. "That was some fun."

29

Her third year was a little easier. Not so many people did the wild doubletake when they figured out she was the skipper. At least two other women had taken the test and passed. One had a boat and the other acted as second captain for some of the longer fishing trips.

Many of Jessie's passengers were repeats so it looked like she would keep her job of captaining a boat as Neddie Rose was very happy with her. The main office had large photographs of the various boats in Neddie Rose's fleet, along with a brief description and picture of the captains. Jessie being a woman was very distinctive. But having a lot of repeat customers showed that Jessie did a good job helping the fishermen have good days. People were signing up to sail with her not just for the novelty, but because she had good results.

However, Donny was gone and this year she had a new deckhand. Skip was a high school junior and was the son of another captain. He knew the business and required very little training. Jessie was unusual because she expected the deck to be clean at all times so Skip was hosing down the deck off and on all day when the scales and/or guts got onto the deck. It made for better footing. Jessie's boat was always neat and clean.

About midseason, on a sunny calm day, Skip was netting a fairly good sized salmon for a customer and trying not to bump the man standing next to him. Jessie had the boat stopped and was talking with a man who was in the cabin with her, who was more interested in the mechanics of the boat than fishing at the moment. Skip was hollering at a fisherman to lead the salmon so it could be netted. Things seemed pretty normal. Everyone had at least one fish and the fishing was good. There was still another hour or so to continue fishing so everyone was happy.

Then one of the fishermen lurched over to a bench and sat down hard, clutching his chest. His fishing partner called to him and asked if he was ok. The man said he was hurting and was having trouble breathing. Jessie put the boat into neutral and was out in a flash.

"You're Bob, right?" He nodded. "What's happening?" she asked.

He looked at her with white pinched lips, still clutching his chest. "I have chest pain and am not breathing too well," he gasped.

"O.K.," she told him. "I'll call the Coast Guard for medical help. You stay on that bench. If you get dizzy, sit on the floor. You understand me?" He nodded. His fishing buddy was now on the bench with him and he nodded also. She looked at his buddy. "If he does decide to sit on the floor, have him lie down and get his feet elevated. I'll find some blankets to keep him warm now. This make sense to you?" Her first aid training had popped into her head. If a person is in shock, they need their feet elevated and to be kept warm. Having a heart attack might cause shock. She didn't know, but wanted to be on the safe side.

"Poles up!" she called to the rest of the customers and quickly stepped into the cabin. She grabbed the emergency radio mike and said, "Coast Guard Station Grays Harbor. This is the **Blue Waters** reporting a medical emergency." She waited and within a few seconds a voice replied, "This is Coast Guard Station Grays Harbor. What is your medical emergency?"

"Strong chest pains and trouble breathing."

"O.K.," the Coast Guard replied. Give me your location."

"Forty-eight latitude ……. And twenty-five longitude ………….. Yellow boat," she replied.

"Our helicopter is on the way and could arrive within 30 minutes. Please switch to channel 23 now."

Jessie switched the channel to 23 and said, "Station Grays Harbor?"

This is Station Grays Harbor. How many people do you have on board?"

"Two crew members, the ailing man and nine others."

"Have life-jackets on everyone and be prepared for the wash of the 'copter when it arrives," the voice replied.

The customers had their lines in and were milling around the man. One lady was trying to hold his hand and was chattering in a high pitched voice and was obviously upset. Bob groaned and let himself down from the bench and sat on the deck. His buddy had him lie down flat and put his feet up on a lunch box he had. He adjusted the blankets.

The lady's voice went even shriller. Jessie approached her and told her to go into the cabin and sit on the bench next to the sink. The woman looked at Jessie and did not seem to understand. Firmly, Jessie pulled her up to her feet and pointed her to the cabin. "Go in and sit on the bench next to the sink," and gave the woman a nudge. She seemed very confused but she went in and sat on the bench.

"Skip," she called and he appeared immediately.

"We need to get everyone into a life-jacket and into the cabin. All of the loose stuff on the deck needs to be stowed somewhere where it won't blow away. The wash from the helicopter can knock people over and it sure can blow away our buckets and poles. You understand?" she asked.

He nodded.

"First the life jackets and then we'll get everyone into the cabin. You can get the loose stuff stowed then."

The people who had been near enough to hear Jessie's command to the deckhand had already found the life-jackets and were handing them around to everyone. Jessie found one and put it on and then knelt down next to Bob. "We need to get a lifejacket on you, Bob. The Coast Guard is going to be here in a few minutes." His buddy helped Jessie gently put the life jacket on Bob. "You need a life-jacket also, Steve," she said to his buddy.

"Sure thing," he said and quickly found a life-jacket and put it on.

"Everyone in the cabin now," she called out. "The wind from the helicopter, when it hovers over us, is really strong. It can knock you down. So, get into the cabin and stay there until the 'copter is gone. The customers seemed a little confused and unsure what to do, but they all started into the cabin."

The helicopter could be heard when it was several miles away. The distinctive whap whap whap was like none other. Jessie's emergency radio crackled and a voice said, "**Blue Waters. Blue Waters.**" Jessie was at her radio. "This is the Blue Waters."

"We will be over your boat in about five minutes. Is the patient conscious?"

"Yes. Breathing erratically, but conscious."

"We will lower our EMT and a basket. You will need to let the basket hit the deck before you secure it.

"Roger that," Jessie answered.

"We will be there shortly."

The 'copter was soon above the boat and Jessie and Steve, Bob's buddy, were next to Bob, protecting him from the wash as best they could. The lead rope was being pulled across the deck. Skip caught it and guided the basket with the EMT in it onto the deck. The EMT hopped onto the deck and moved the basket over near to Bob. He knelt down and talked briefly to Bob while checking his pulse. Bob was replying in short grunts but obviously knew what was happening. The EMT and Steve put Bob into the basket very gingerly. The EMT hopped back into the basket and gave a thumbs up motion to the helicopter pilot. The basket began to rise and soon they were both in the 'copter and it began its return flight.

"That sure doesn't take long," Skip said as he watched it disappear.

Jessie returned to the radio. "Thank you, Station Grays Harbor. Over."

The boat passengers were a little subdued and the quiet was extra quiet with the noise and confusion of the helicopter being gone.

"Where will they take him?" Steve asked.

"To the hospital in Hoquiam. He will be there in a few minutes," Jessie said.

"I'd like to get back and be with him. I'll let his family know what is happening also."

"O.K." She turned to the rest of the fishermen. "We are going to return to port now. If you want an adjustment or rebate, talk with the office. I'm sure they will understand."

Most of the people smiled and shook their head. They began to shed their life-jackets. "This has been pretty interesting," one of them said.

Jessie returned to the captain's chair and turned the boat towards Westport and headed home. "Another day, another dollar," she thought to herself. "You just never know what is going to happen."

And so ended another day of fishing.

30

Jessie was settled into her fishing schedule for the summer. She was at her dad's house babysitting Sam. Supper was over and her dad and Betty were gone for the evening. Sam had legos and was trying to build a ship. Jessie wasn't much help but enjoyed watching his efforts.

"You get to stay up until 10 tonight, Sam." She pushed a lincoln log over to help in a coming up gap. "No school tomorrow."

"You like school?" she asked him.

"I know my colors," he replied.

Jessie laughed. Sam was having a ball at school. He didn't like having a sitter and it was hard to get a straight answer out of him.

"Your colors, huh," she said flatly and laughed some more.

Just then the phone rang. She went over and answered it.

"Martin residence."

"Jessie?" a voice asked.

"Yes," said Jessie. Surprise in her voice.

"This is Ben Major. I called your apartment and was told you were there."

"Oh." Jessie was surprised. Ben owned the Deep Sea Charter Company. She hadn't talked to him in over three years.

"Is this a good time to talk or am I catching you being busy?" he asked.

"This is fine. Sam doesn't need to get ready for bed for another couple of hours." She paused. "What's up?"

"Well, Jim Masters is looking for a new captain for his ship. You might remember her, the "**Sea Explorer**?""

Jessie remembered her well. She was in good shape and a fairly large boat. Bigger than the **Blue Waters**, for sure.

"Yes. I remember her," Jessie said.

"Well. Kevin suggested I get you to captain her. We'd like you back with Deep Sea Charters. We need a Captain Martin here somehow."

Jessie was amazed. She could make more money being the skipper of a bigger boat. "Of course," she said. "I'd be honored."

"Come by my office tomorrow after work and we can settle some of the details. Kevin tells me you have become a first-class captain. High praise from that old coot."

Jessie laughed. "You might be careful, Ben. Someone may have bribed him to come up with this."

Jessie thought for a moment. This is what she had been working towards ever since she had the notion to get her captain's license. She was good at her work and she had proven it. And she was being recognized for it. She smiled to herself. "Dad is going to love hearing this. This is what we were hoping for when I took that first job with him as a deckhand." She smiled to herself again. "And Mom is going to be amazed …. But proud."

"Hey, Sam. I've just been offered a bigger boat.

Sam looked up. He was preteen but remembered well his dad's time as a salmon boat captain. "You must be just a chip off the old block." He grinned at Jessie. "Way to go, Sis."

About the Author

Carolyn Jean Selch, Jean to her friends, was born in Grand Junction, Colorado, and raised her three children, Ray, Kelly and Glen in Steamboat Springs. She is a graduate of Mesa State College and the University of Northern Colorado.

Jean and her husband, Ralph, decided to retire to Washington State along the coast. She met Jenny Leighton when both played cello for the Grays Harbor Symphony. They carpooled and over several years, the stories Jenny told Jean about Jenny's younger years in the recreational salmon fishing industry, totally intrigued Jean.

"Jenny you need to write a book about your adventures." "Writing is not my thing," Jenny replied. So, Jean decided to write this book about Jenny's entering the men's world of the recreational salmon fishing industry. All of her accomplishments depicted in this book are accurate.

Acknowledgements

Many thanks to Jenny Leighton who shared her stories about her career as a sea captain.

She reviewed numerous manuscripts as the book was being written to help keep the stories fairly accurate.

Loving thanks to Lindell Stacey-Horton for the beautiful seascape she specifically painted for the cover of this book.'

Kudos to daughter-in-law, Claudia Marsh, for the photographs of the seascape.

And, lastly, and mostly, thanks to husband, Ralph, for several years of help and encouragement while this book was being hatched.

Jenny's History

Jenny, aka Jessie, began deckhanding for her dad when she was 15 years old. She worked on various boats for five years as a deckhand, gaining experience and the sea time required to take and pass the Coast Guard test which, a few days before her 21st birthday, granted her the capacity "License to Operate or Navigate Passenger Carrying vessels, which after more testing , and experience on the water, was upgraded to :master of Near Coastal Steam or Motor Vessels of Not More Than 100 Gross Tons."

Jenny took passengers to fish for salmon or bottom fish, and also ran gray whale watch trips out of Westport, Washington. She captained two passenger ferries between Westport and Ocean Shores. She worked on orca watch trips out of Everett, Washington. She also ran and hired on as 2nd captain on albacore tuna trips out of Westport.

Jenny retired from fishing and boats in 2009.

Currently, Jenny has more time for her other passion... music ... playing the cello in the Grays Harbor Symphony, also playing cello and piano for local pit orchestras, and, most fun of all, playing piano in the Celtic fusion duo "Captain's Daughter".